Kick
in the
h*e*ad

Melissa,

Thanks for coming and
listening - I'll sing
at the next pos
party!

Love
Steve

STORIES BY

Kick in the head

STEVEN RINEHART

Doubleday

New York London Toronto Sydney Auckland

PUBLISHED BY DOUBLEDAY a division of Random House, Inc. 1540 Broadway, New York, New York 10036 • DOUBLEDAY and the portrayal of an anchor with a dolphin are trademarks of Doubleday, a division of Random House, Inc. • The following stories have previously appeared and are reprinted by permission of the author: "Make Me," *Harpers*, September 1995 • "The Order of the Arrow," *Ploughshares*, Fall 1995 • "Outstanding in My Field," GQ, May 1994 • "Burning Luv," *Story*, Fall 1993 • "Funny Cars," *Black Warrior Review*, Fall/Winter 1990 • "LeSabre," *Georgia Review*, Spring 1998

Book design by Nicola Ferguson

Library of Congress Cataloging-in-Publication Data
Rinehart, Steven.
Kick in the head: stories / by Steven Rinehart.—1st ed.
p.   cm.
1. United States—Social life and customs—20th century—Fiction.
2. Psychological fiction, American.   3. Men—Psychology—Fiction.   I. Title.
PS3568.I564 K5 2000
813'.54—dc21   99-055774

ISBN 0-385-49853-5

1   3   5   7   9   10   8   6   4   2

First Edition

For Verle Rinehart (1932–1998),

and for my mother

Acknowledgments

These stories represent what sometimes seems to be several lifetimes of work, none of which would have been possible without the generous help of the following people: Elizabeth Cuthrell, Phil Damon, Madison Smartt Bell, Geoff Becker, Fred Leebron, Eric Simonoff, Deb Futter, and especially Barbara Jones.

Support and funding were also provided by the Copernicus Society and James Michener, the National Endowment for the Arts, the Virginia Center for the Creative Arts, and Jeannie and Bernie Jacobsen.

Contents

Kick
in the
head

make
me

On the sixth day of her hunger strike Lydia Martinez entered my dreams and immediately died there. She died so convincingly that I awoke and for a few moments could not imagine her alive again. I had to force it. I forced it and then I saw her, behind a Bunsen burner, her pretty face framed inside her black hair and lit by the lapping yellow flame. I felt better, much better, but as much as I tried I could not fall asleep again. Lydia was not just any girl; besides being the brightest, she was my One and Only—the one and only student I was allowed to think about in that way I thought about her.

"Do you know what day it is?" I asked Pearl the next morning in the teachers' lounge, over a cigarette. Pearl was my ex-girlfriend—an English teacher. Through an arrangement the two of us shared, she was allowed to think about Gabriel, her One and Only. Gabriel was Lydia's former boyfriend and the reason for the girl's hunger strike. Think only, Pearl and I had agreed, that way no one gets hurt. At least, that was the way it had started.

Pearl blew smoke out her nostrils. "How could I not know?" she said. "She stage-whispers it to him every day in

3

homeroom: 'I'm on Day Five, Gabriel,' she says, 'Day Six to-day.' She's got him worried to death."

"He didn't seem particularly worried in Earth Science to-day," I said. "But just for the record, it's Day Seven. Seven days since you drove the boy home."

Pearl blew a mouthful of smoke at the dirty window that overlooked two granite benches donated by the Class of '78. The windows in the teachers' lounge were never cleaned. The janitors refused, the teachers refused. No one else was al-lowed inside.

Then Pearl was looking at me with tears balanced in the corners of her eyes, a device she had always used to great ef-fect. "Chris, I'm just barely making it," she said. "Sometimes I think I'm not going to make it. I know it's not the smart thing to do, but I'm just barely hanging on. A skin of the teeth kind of thing. Do you know what I mean?"

"Oh, Pearl." My voice was more tender than I wanted it to be. "Don't be dramatic. He's just a boy, think about it."

"That's the trouble—it's all I think about." She laughed, but the laugh had dislodged the tears and so she couldn't fol-low up on it.

"Anyway," she said, "it's not like I expect you to know what I'm talking about." She sniffed out another laugh and then sighed. "I'm really very sorry I said that."

"Forget it," I said, but the pit of my stomach had gone cold. There was a pause and after a moment I filled it. "If nothing else, consider Lydia."

She snorted. "I don't give two shits about Lydia and her stupid hunger strikes. She'll quit just like the other times. She always eats eventually."

"No," I said, "she never just quits. Gabriel always comes back to her, then she eats. That's not the same as quitting."

"She'll quit this time. I'll bet you anything she's eating by Friday."

I didn't say anything for a moment, then I rubbed my eyes hard. "I'm having trouble sleeping," I said.

"Again?" Pearl mashed the nose of her cigarette in the center of the ashtray. It stayed there, bent and broken, its pink end in the air.

"Why do they humor her?" she said. "They should yank her out of school when she pulls this stuff. It's only for the attention. They should just yank her out for her own good."

Outside the dirty window some stray papers blew across the grass. A girl shrieked and a bad muffler blatted into the distance.

"Who's they?" I said.

had only kissed Lydia, and I had only done it once. It happened last week on Parents' Night. Lydia's father—of all people— had sought me out at the front lab station where I was explaining the Periodic Table to a single mom whose child was nowhere to be found. He drew up behind me and out of the corner of my eye I could see him shifting his weight from foot to foot. Lydia hung back in the doorway and watched us, her chin low to her chest.

"What is this about?" he asked, when the woman had left. He waved a paper in front of my eyes.

I took the paper from him and read it. It took two passes before I recognized it.

"Advanced lab takes some extra equipment," I said, handing it back. "It's just a deposit. If nothing is broken it's all refunded at the end of the semester."

He examined the paper doubtfully. Lydia turned her face away from the room.

"Just in time for Christmas," I added. By then the vice principal had noticed the scene developing from his office across the hall, where he was entertaining a man in an army uniform. He glanced at Lydia and then frowned at me. The man in the uniform spoke to him but the vice principal continued frowning through the doorway.

"Your son Franco?" I said a bit louder. "He's a very bright boy. A good student."

"I pay this already," he said, staring at the paper. He had started to look panicked. "Already pay."

The vice principal circled around the man in the uniform to be closer. "Yes," I said, taking it from him, "I remember getting it. No problem."

Lydia's father nodded with relief and turned to leave. He was almost at the door and then he stiffened and took Lydia by the arm and pulled her back to me. She was pale. Her black hair fell into her face, as if she were hiding behind it. The vice principal escaped from the man in uniform and stood right in the doorway next to my poster of the Curies. He stood with his nose slightly in the air, sniffing scandal.

"This," Lydia's father said. "This is my daughter."

I nodded at him. My hands went in and out of my pockets.

"My daughter," he said again. He was starting to look angry.

"Yes," I said. Madame Curie and the vice principal stared at me.

"Not my son. Not Franco."

"Yes, of course," I said in a rush. "My mistake. Also taken care of. No problem, Mr. Martinez." When I said his name he nodded at me and let go of Lydia's arm. The fabric of her sleeve remained puckered where he had gripped her. He walked out the door and Lydia followed behind, brushing past the vice principal, who had been collared once again by the old soldier. She never looked up.

At half past nine I snapped the locks shut on my briefcase and closed the door to the classroom behind me. Pearl had long ago left, and I walked across the varsity diamond to the teachers' parking lot. When I reached it Lydia was sitting on the trunk of my car with her feet on the bumper. Her hands were pressed between her knees and her hair fell on either side of her face.

"Gabriel went off with her," she said, not looking up. "Why didn't you stop them?"

"It's nothing," I said. "There's nothing to worry about." I was too tired and too disappointed to think about Pearl anymore. She and I had had our big scene just a few days before. My feelings and faults were still freshly exhumed and lingered about me like an unpleasant odor. I put my briefcase down and sat on the trunk next to Lydia. I thought of five or six things to say but instead I leaned over, moved her hair, and kissed her. She didn't raise her head and I almost missed her pretty mouth. I kept my face next to hers for a moment and then I straightened up.

"It's all so disappointing," she said. She pulled her knees up to her chin.

I felt my face heat up stupidly. "What is?" I said.

"Everything," she said. "Just everything."

"Well, you don't have to worry, I won't do that again."

She finally raised her head but I couldn't see her eyes in the shadows. She didn't say anything for a moment while she looked at me. Then she turned away. "See what I mean?" she said.

On the way home we stopped by the Dairy Queen for an ice cream. She barely touched her cone; I left her a block from her house with it dripping down around her fist.

That, as far as I knew, was the last time she ate.

On Day Eight, in Earth Science, Gabriel was napping in the last row when the two AV drones, twin brothers with twin eyeglasses, wheeled in the TV and VCR. Gabriel's head lay sideways on his arms, a mass of soft black curls. As soon as the video started he jerked his head up and wiped the back of his hand across his lips. It was a film about cellular mitosis. When they showed a rabbit being inseminated and then sacrificed, he leapt to his feet.

"You mean they killed it?" he cried. "What is this, Mr. Bergman, some kind of bunny snuff film?"

"Gabriel," I said. I was always tempted to stop there, at just the recitation of his name, but he was one of those people who was affirmed by his name being spoken aloud, just the way others were diminished. It was like food to him, and I didn't like seeing him fed in my class.

I stopped the film. "Gabriel, the term is sacrifice, not kill. We've been over this."

"Kill is kill, Mr. Bergman," he said. "Dead is dead."

"This is about life beginning," I said. "I really think that if you'd just sit down and watch, you'll be interested."

"I don't know," he said doubtfully. "There's the whole eye for an eye thing . . ."

"Sit down, Gabriel."

Gabriel sat down, somehow larger and more beautiful. I started the film. When the egg finally divided—the chromosomes cleaving and rushing to their opposite poles—the class twisted in their seats to look back at him. He was asleep, his head on his arms. The remainder of the film seemed interminable.

"Pearl," I told her that night at her kitchen table, "you're

9

crossing the line. I don't know what else to say to you. Think of Tess of the Whatshernames, think of Sister Goddamn Carrie."

But it was too late; just then I realized that she had already gone through with it. She was glowing, but trying to hide it.

"Wrong sex, to begin with," she said. She fingered her faux pearl strand, her trademark. She didn't realize the pearls rode too far up the nape of her neck and emphasized her slightly hunched shoulders and sallow coloring. I had told her once that she reminded me of Garbo, but not the reason why.

"Let me show you something," she said. "You aren't going to believe this." She crossed her yellow kitchen and brought back a tin canister. Inside was white sugar, polluted with what looked to be tiny brown crumbs.

"He puts sugar on absolutely everything. Toast, covered with butter, covered with sugar. Can you believe it?" She licked her finger and poked it into the canister. She held it up in front of her, coated. "Not a single cavity in his entire head. Teeth of steel." After a moment she wiped the finger on the tablecloth.

"Lydia Martinez fainted in Kaplan's class," I said in a calm voice.

She stood up quickly and ran water over her hands. "I'm not going to feel guilty. It has nothing to do with me." She rubbed her hands on a dish towel.

"I had a dream she was dead. I mean a nightmare. I haven't slept since."

"You told me this already."

"I called her house. Her parents pretended not to understand English. They put her little brother on and he called me a whore-lover and hung up."

She examined her pearls absently. "They thought you were selling something. Did you say who you were?"

"When she came to, she asked them what day it was. Kaplan told her Tuesday. He didn't know what she meant."

"God, would you listen to yourself," she said. "Why don't you just admit you want to sleep with the girl and get it over with."

My hand gripped the tablecloth. "Don't make fun of me."

"Jesus," she said. "I didn't say you had to do it, I just said that you should admit it. It would be good for you."

I stood up. The tablecloth was crumpled where I had grasped it. "You're not exactly the expert on what would be good for me, are you?"

Pearl rolled her eyes. "Then why did you come over here? To show me what a Tough Time you're having?"

"To help you, although now I can't remember why." I picked up her sugar canister and dumped it on the table. "Maybe it was so you could tell me the fascinating sugar anecdote. Got any spiral notebooks to show me? Gym socks to hold under my nose?"

She said something but I was already moving toward the

door. The screen slapped shut behind me, followed quickly by the slam of the interior door. I dropped the keys putting them in the door lock and then again putting them in the ignition. I drove past Lydia's house on the way home.

By Day Eleven Lydia's skin had taken on a milky, mother-of-pearl glow. She didn't seem thin as much as translucent. Her face was serenity itself—her glance at the wall clock was serenity, her gaze at the classroom door was serenity, her entire aspect, watching me, serenity. I explained quantum theory to the class the way it had been explained to me. I understood the loathing in their eyes.

After class I locked the door and turned out the lights. I laid my fingers gently on the bones of Lydia's hand.

"Did you understand that?" I asked. "Do I make any sense?"

"No," she said. "It's kind of like Mass, except without God, without any feelings."

I put pressure on her hand. "Lydia, you're losing muscle by now. You're losing calcium. Look at the Periodic Table. That's not just rocks and metal, that's you."

"Jesus fasted for forty days and forty nights."

I shook my head. "If he really did that, he was just looking to make a big splash." I could feel her tiny Catholic pulse quicken in the back of her hand.

"Have you ever fasted?" she asked.

"No."

"It reminds you that we're all just tubes, you know. In and out. I know that sounds disgusting but it's funny; when you don't eat, nothing sounds disgusting the way it usually does. Everything seems so clean."

"It's an illusion," I said. "I can explain the chemistry behind it."

"I know you can but not now, okay?"

"Okay," I said.

"It's like this," she said. "I lived for Gabriel, and now he's gone. Why should I keep going if what I lived for is gone?"

I lifted my hand. "You say that because you like the way it sounds."

"You see?" she said. "I try to tell you but you don't believe me." Then she took my hand back and her grip was strong. "It's not that I want to think about him; I don't want to think about him. I just want someone to think about me." She raised her hand and put the ends of my fingers against her lips. My arm hung heavy and limp between us.

"You know," she whispered, "you could make me want to stop." I could feel the breath from each syllable on my fingertips. "Why don't you just make me?"

"I dreamt that you died," I said. "I haven't slept since. Isn't that enough?"

But it wasn't. She sighed her disappointed sigh and looked at the clock above the door. She stood up, dropping my hand. I stood up to follow her but she was already gone; after all, it was Friday afternoon and the week was over for the likes of me.

That night on the phone Pearl spoke with the kitchen tap running in the background.

"What is this," I said. "Now you think your phone is bugged?"

"Of course not. It just makes me feel better."

"From this end it sounds like you're being gassed."

She laughed too loudly. "What a clever thing to say. You're such a wit."

"He's there, isn't he?" I said. "And you're afraid he'll hear? Where is he, on the couch?"

"No. Guess again."

"I don't have to guess again. He's on the couch, watching television. You're pretending to like it. 'What is this show about?' you ask him. 'Now, who is he, I forget who she is.' You ask him every five seconds if he wants something to drink. You make the mistake of talking during some murder or explosion and he tells you to fuck off why don't you."

The water rushed louder. "You listen to me," she said.

I waited but all I heard was the water. "I'm listening."

"Be quiet a second." Her hand went over the receiver. When the water noise came back I could hear her breath.

"I have to go," she whispered.

Before I could answer, the water stopped. Pearl's voice lightened artificially. "Okay, Chris, I'll see you on Monday. I'll be sure to bring that book."

"Fuck," I yelled into the mouthpiece. "Fuck." It was loud

enough for him to hear; loud enough if she hadn't covered the earpiece on the way to the cradle.

arth Science, bonehead science, science for simpletons. Monday, Day Fourteen, and Gabriel sat in the front row. He yawned twice; once for real and once for me. He wasn't wearing socks. He had a seventeen-year-old's silly weekend peach-fuzz beard. He scratched himself. The girl in the next seat watched him with sad but hopeful virginity.

"What I want to know, Mr. Bergman," Gabriel said, "is why animals don't like intercourse. They always scream."

Titters. "Gabriel . . ."

"Cats act like they're being killed."

"I don't know that that's true."

"It is. It's a nightmare. Sometimes they get stuck together." More titters. "No, seriously, they do."

I tried a stern tone. "We're not talking about reproduction anymore, Gabriel. That was last week. Pay attention."

"I want to review. I didn't get it all the first time."

I sighed. "Neither did I, Gabriel, but life goes on."

"Mr. Bergman," he said. "Good one."

"Who knows what phloem is?" I asked, over his head.

Gabriel cleared his throat noisily and the class tittered again. But he was through. He was, after all, exhausted.

Fifty minutes later Pearl stood in the teachers' lounge

swirling coffee in a stained Styrofoam cup. There were no stir-
rers; there hadn't been for weeks. I usually used a Bic.

"Your young man is practically passed out," I said. "If he
can't practice he'll get his seventeen-year-old butt chewed."

"Too late." She put her cup down and attempted an evil
grin that ended up a tired leer.

"Lydia Martinez—"

She put both hands to her ears. "Stop," she said. "It's not
even ten o'clock, Chris. Give me a morning's peace, why
don't you?"

"—is in the nurse's office. She fainted in Kaplan's class
again. He's beside himself. I heard him on the phone to his
wife; I think he was crying."

"He's on Lithium, for Christ's sake. The man weeps when
the cafeteria runs out of Tater Tots."

"What about your job," I said. "What about your career?"

"God," she said. "If you had any kind of heart."

"We had this conversation, remember? Everyone's not
like you two, you know."

Her mouth wrinkled. "Oh, yes, I forgot. The chaste virgin.
You wouldn't believe the things Gabriel says he's done with
her."

"I'm not interested."

"Then why are you so pale all of a sudden?" She closed
her eyes for a second. "Look, I'm sorry but you started it."

"I told you I haven't been sleeping. I'm starting to see
flashing lights out of the corners of my eyes. Whispering
voices. I haven't had that since college."

Her eyes flickered with concern, but just barely. "No sleep for two weeks?"

"I don't have the dreams, at least, but I still can't sleep."

"Is this about me? Chris, I gave you chances. I gave you chances until I couldn't give anymore."

"I don't need chances," I said. "I've got more chances than I can cope with right now."

Just then the vice principal stepped in through the door. We stared at him. He wrinkled his nose and stepped back out. The vice principal got his coffee from the ladies in the office. He had either wanted to use the teachers' bathroom or wanted to locate the two of us, establish our whereabouts. The expression on his face fit either scenario.

We waited for fifteen seconds, picked up our briefcases, and left in opposite directions for second period.

The vice principal had been hired the previous fall. Before he arrived there had been both a vice principal and a dean of students. Soon afterward they canned the dean of students and gave his duties to the new vice principal. It was obvious that he considered this some kind of promotion and not a screwing like the rest of us did, so from then on everyone figured him to be either an idiot or a zealous bureaucrat and avoided him altogether. The whole thing ended up making him bitter and suspicious and awfully good at his job.

The vice principal's office walls were lined with books that he had swiped from the library; they still had the cellophane sleeves with decimal codes typed on white strips across the bottoms of the spines. He kept a football on a wooden stand on his desk; it had a leather satchel handle sewn onto the laces. He had been a coach of some kind at his last school and this was a gift from his players, young men who had apparently adored him. The students at our school were constantly stealing it. When they weren't stealing his football with the handle, they were writing his name on the paper bottoms of butter pats along with an obscenity and then tossing them up to the ceiling of the cafeteria, where they would stick. Every once in a while without warning one dropped, like a dead thing, onto someone's food.

"Mr. Bergman," he said, leaning back in his gray vinyl chair. "We have a couple of situations. At least two that I know about."

The little lights flashed in the dark corners, where the bookshelves met. I shook my head a little to clear it.

"We have an emotionally unbalanced student on our hands and, I believe, a troubled instructor. A very troubled instructor."

"Teacher," I said, a little distractedly.

"I beg your pardon?"

"We have teaching certificates, not instructing certificates. I'm not a lifeguard."

"Yes, I'm aware that you're not. I wonder if—"

"I'm sorry," I said quickly. "I haven't been sleeping."

"I beg your pardon?" He had leaned forward in his chair.

"I don't sleep. It's as simple as that. Please continue with what you were saying."

"Fine. I thought I should tell you that the Superintendent

18

of Schools has been enquiring about Lydia Martinez." He said that, the bastard: enquiring.

"Well, when she dies he'll probably stop enquiring. Not right away, but eventually."

"You're close to her," he said without a beat. "She's in your sixth period." His face showed no hint of accusation, not really.

"And now you want me to shoot myself in the foot. Isn't that a term you people use? Shoot yourself in the foot?"

"Not really," he said calmly. "I want you to get your girlfriend to talk to her, that's all." He picked up his football, not by the handle but by one blunt end, as if he were fondling a breast. The late afternoon sun suddenly appeared through the window behind him, and I had to lean a bit to the side to avoid getting it full in the face. It struck the vice principal halfway through the back of his head; his face darkened and his right ear glowed red around the edges.

"To think," he said, staring at his football. "We give them films about VD, about HIV, but we don't mention this danger at all."

"What danger?" He was trying to confuse me, I knew it.

"Tragic," he said.

I closed my eyes, the easier to block out the sun. "All right," I said. "What do you want her to say?"

He looked up at me. There was no triumph in his expression. "Frankly, I don't know."

"Then what would satisfy you?"

"Calories," he said. "An orange, a pear. A carrot stick. The goddamn Apple Brown Betty would do, but I don't recommend it." Levity. He smiled at his own joke. He was smart, though, I had to give that to him. She would listen to Pearl; more than to anyone else, she would listen to Pearl.

"Okay," I said. It sounded inadequate but I was tired from not sleeping.

"Good," he said. "Kaplan will be happier."

"I beg your pardon?"

He flashed an innocent smile. "Our troubled teacher. I have a feeling this will perk him up."

For a second I was stunned. You're priceless, I thought. Still, long after we're gone you'll be here. There was some logic in that.

I started to get up to leave, but I sat back down. "Before I go," I said, "what danger were you referring to?"

"Oh, I thought it was obvious." He put the football back on its stand. "Mental illness." He tapped his forehead for emphasis.

"She's not mentally ill. She actually has a point if you listen to her."

"I wasn't referring to her. She'll come around. It's all for the attention, I'm sure." He looked at my face and smiled. "Kaplan," he said, "of course."

"Of course," I repeated. I left him there in his little slant of sunlight, behind his football.

"Fuck him," Pearl said, back in the teachers' lounge. "Why should I?"

"It's the right thing to do," I said. "You owe it to her."

"You need help, Chris. You need real help. Haven't you been paying attention to what's going on here?"

"Don't start. This isn't about me."

"No, of course not," she said. "Never about you."

"I told him you'd do it. I think he suspects something with you and Gabriel."

"Jesus," she said. "Did you bother to ask him why he had to involve you, then? Didn't you wonder about that?"

"Look, like it or not, he's actually right. All you have to do is talk to her. She'll listen to you."

"God," she said. She closed her eyes and shook her head. "This is something that should be begged."

My heart pounded and the lights flashed. "You're crazy. I'm doing you the favor. I covered for you."

When Pearl opened her eyes she looked at me calmly. "If I talk to her, I tell her everything," she said.

"Tell her anything," I said. "Tell her I have no heart. Tell her I beat you. Tell her the truth if you have to. Tell her whatever it was you told yourself. Just talk to her. This is me begging."

She sighed and looked out the dirty window. "Where and when?" she said. "Let's get it over with."

Pearl sat in the driver's seat. Lydia sat in the passenger's. I watched them from the bleachers of the varsity diamond. When they were done Pearl drove off and Lydia stood alone under the trees by right field. It had gotten dark fast and the streetlights were already on. She stood for a few moments and then walked over to me.

21

"I feel scraped out," she said. Her glance was feathery; she was fighting hard to concentrate. I wondered if she saw the flashing lights like I did.

"Is she always like that?" she asked.

"Yes," I said. "But maybe not so much anymore."

She sat for a moment. "She told me to tell you something. I don't know if I should."

I shook my head. "I want to know what she told you."

"She told me to tell you this first."

"All right. If you want to."

"She said to tell you that she doesn't feel sorry for you anymore."

"She's smart," I said. Some white flashes went off and I had to close my eyes for a second.

"Everyone says you two used to be in love. Were you in love with her?"

"No," I said. "What else did she say?"

"Is it true I got you in trouble? You might lose your job?"

I almost laughed. I could have made that up myself. "Maybe," I said.

"And everything would be okay if I just ate?"

"Yes, it would." I was lying so quickly now, so easily; lying to impress a seventeen-year-old girl. Her martyr, her hero.

"I didn't want to hurt anybody," she said.

"Lydia, I need to know," I said. "Did she say anything else?"

Her lips went tight. "She said that she's never going to give him up."

The flashing lights again. "Anything else?"

"She said I should help you and be with you. That it's important."

My heart sank. Oh, Pearl. Then the streetlight behind me came on and suddenly Lydia's face was lit and stayed lit and I could finally see it, the whole of it. Her skin glowed; I wanted to touch it with the backs of my fingers. I did.

"Lydia," I said. "You remember what you said to me before, about making you? I could do that. I could just make you."

But then that familiar resigned look crept in, very adult on her seventeen-year-old face, and I knew I was too late. "It sounds all right now," she said, "but what about in a couple of days? You might feel different."

"I won't," I said. "I won't ever feel different."

She looked away, moving her face in front of the street lamp. Blocked now, it scattered its light into the air surrounding her head.

"I might, you see?" she said. She turned back to me and I knew that despite what Pearl had told her, she had seen something. I could tell she felt immensely sorry for me, maybe even contemptuous; it was all over her perfect face.

"It's just that I never know how I'll feel after I start eating again," she said. "I might start eating and then it would all seem bad and I'd never want to see you again."

Then for God's sake, don't eat, I wanted to say. I'd rather you disappeared. I'd rather the earth opened and swallowed you whole. I'd rather you were dead.

"What would you do then?" she asked, her eyes suddenly bright and sharp and piercing. She took my hand and squeezed my fingers hard, down near the ends. "What would you do if that happened?"

My chest kicked and then went hollow. "That's not what's important," I said. "What's most important is that you eat and get better."

In the light from the street it seemed that this time disappointment filled her whole thin face, as if she had taken it in in one gigantic gulp.

"That's what everyone keeps telling me," she said. "And that's exactly why I can't."

She sat there on the bleachers, flashes going off all around her, and I put my arm around her. It hung, limp, off her shoulder. I knew that I wanted to do more than put my arm around her, that I wanted to kiss her right there on the varsity diamond bleachers in front of God and the vice principal and Madame Curie and everybody, but I didn't right then, I didn't.

the
order
of the
arrow

Heitman, the homosexual, the insane, is my tentmate. Again. Porter, the fat kid who cries a lot, cried again this morning, saying he didn't want to tent with Heitman ever again. Last night Heitman put ticks on Porter's eyelashes while he slept. This morning our scoutmaster, Casper, had to pluck them off with tweezers, since the hot-match trick was too dangerous that close to his eyeball. The ticks came away with tiny chunks of Porter's eyelid clasped in their jaws, like grains of sand. Casper said this was good; if the head stayed in, Porter could lose the eye. He told Heitman one more time and he was out. As soon as he left the tent, Heitman dropped his pants and pretended to masturbate violently in Casper's direction.

Two nights ago Heitman leapt off his cot in the middle of the night and onto my back, bucking frantically. "Bergie," he cried, "Oh, Bergie, Bergie, Bergie, you hunk of man." I tried to curl up and beat him off with my fists, but he knew where to put his knees.

"You bastard," I cried, "get off me," but Heitman was laughing and slapping the back of my head.

"We're buddies, aren't we?" Heitman said. "Say we're

hunch buddies, Bergman. Hunch buddies forever." He stopped suddenly, before I could say anything, and got off me. I turned over and saw that the moon was out and shining through the fabric of the roof. Heitman was half dressed. He stood bent over, peering out the front flap of the tent. His shoelaces were untied and his shirt was off. He had his Scout neckerchief tucked in the back pocket of his jeans. He turned around, his black hair in his eyes, and said, loud over the crickets, "Let's go out, Bergman. Let's go explore."

eitman," I tell him, "you can't catch fish with your hands. It's impossible." He ignores me and wades out farther into the stream in his underwear, the moonlight reflecting around where his knees disappear into the current. He rises up and sinks down, stepping on hidden shelves and rock formations, not seeming to worry about his balance. He stops on a high spot and squats down, his hands in front of him.

"They're sleeping," he says. "You sneak up on them while they're sleeping." I can see his rounded back and the row of tiny knobs that runs up to his neck. The rippling water of the stream makes his back look strange. It looks striped like a trout, or maybe like he's been whipped.

I settle back and look up at the sky, listening to the screaming of the frogs and crickets. My eyes are just starting to close when something cold and spiny hits me on the throat, falls to the ground, and lies there flipping in the dirt.

Heitman sloshes back to the bank and climbs out. He squats next to the fish. It has stopped moving, its upturned eye brilliantly white against the dark ground. It arches its tail and lets it fall. Its gills open and close and its mouth flexes, the moon reflecting off the edges of its scales. Heitman picks it up and walks over to the water.

"Don't hold it tight," I tell him. "Just let it go easy. If you hold it tight then its scales will rot away." It's something my grandfather told me. He never touched the fish he threw back; he cut his best hooks apart with wire trimmers rather than tear up their mouths. He tried to save the small ones but still when he let them go some just arced over slow and slid away.

Heitman turns and bends sideways at the waist and launches the fish straight up into the sky. It disappears and for a second there is no sound, just the crickets and the rustling water, then the fish hits the ground next to me like a dropped stone. Its body doesn't move but its mouth opens and closes, slower than before. Its eye is now dark and may be gone, I can't tell. I pick it up and walk over to the edge of the stream. The fish is bone-rigid in my hand, frozen in an arc. I bend down and wash the dirt off. But the eye is still black, and I throw it up gently over the water. Seconds later it hits with a small splash, shattering the reflection of the moon, and disappears.

Heitman is furious. "That's fine," he says, shaking water from his arms. "That's just great. Now what do I have to show?" He grabs his pants and starts up the path. He doesn't say a word to me all the way back to camp.

The next day around the steam tables everyone talks about Friday night, the Order of the Arrow ceremony, and if they'll be Tapped Out. The generator is on and Old Willy is watching television under the bus tarp. Old Willy is Casper's father, and he invented the steam tables and the water heater and fixed up the old school bus that takes us around. We know that no other scout troop has an electrical generator, no other troop gets to wear jeans and not wear shirts and smoke cigarettes just about whenever they please. We are lucky. Casper has always preferred a more natural, Indian-style philosophy. According to Casper the old army scouts were just half-ass Indians at best, and he considers most of the standard Boy Scout stuff silly. Summer camp is the only organized camp he lets his troop attend, because of the Order of the Arrow ceremony, where each troop selects a few of its boys to be transformed into men, the way the Indians used to.

"Merit badges are for pussies," Casper says. "Uniforms are for mailmen. I should make you all get tattoos instead." Casper has tattoos, up and down both arms. He wears boots with metal toes. He is a Korean veteran, the seniors say. He has a medal for valor against the enemy, and a scar on his shoulder from a Chinese bayonet. He's tough, but fair, he likes to say. Every kid gets a fair shake.

Casper's right-hand men are the senior troop leaders.

They're in high school and they don't eat with the rest of us, the small ones. The only one of us they can tolerate is Heitman, who they get a charge out of. They've learned that Heitman will do almost anything anyone dares him to do; he eats small animals raw, sets his hair on fire, that kind of thing. He eats at their fire but they won't let him sleep with them in their canopy tent. Heitman has been known to howl at night; an unearthly cry, like rutting hyenas at a fire drill, Casper says. The only time Heitman can be sure not to howl is in my tent, so he mostly sleeps with me. He tells everyone I'm his official hunch buddy, and whatever they think, everybody pretty much leaves me alone. When I walk by they whisper to each other. I know what I am called. I am Heitman's girlfriend.

The seniors spend most of their time sitting around their own fire, smoking cigarettes and telling stories about women they've molested. Chadwell is the biggest. He has removable front teeth and long black hair parted in the middle. In camp he wears feathers in it, two of them that dangle just next to his ear. Sometimes he soots the area under his eyes. Garcia is only slightly smaller, but with bigger shoulders. He sits next to Chadwell and breaks the wood that goes into the fire with his bare hands, sometimes using the arch of his shoulders for leverage. He once hit me in the back of the head for leaving grease in one of the big pots I was cleaning. The next day he came up to me and told me a sex joke which I didn't really get, and I've been friends with him ever since. I give him the cigarettes I steal from my mother but don't smoke.

Heitman has gotten ahold of some Mace from somewhere. His father is a mailman, he says, but I know he's lying. Heitman lives on the street behind mine and everybody on the block knows that his father stays home all day, looking after his chinchillas. Mr. Heitman has a patent on a chinchilla-killing machine that hooks up to a car battery. He calls it the Chilla-Killa. You clamp one end on the chinchilla's nose and stick the other in its anus, then throw the switch. They stiffen right up, Mr. Heitman told me once when I'd come around, right up like a big furry dick. It's not the volts, he said, it's the amps. He shook a dead chinchilla in my face and laughed when I screamed.

We sit on a stone wall by the front gate to the camp, and Heitman hides the Mace behind the wall from a line of scouts who are marching in to use the lake. They're from the rich kids' troop. We're out of uniform so their scoutmaster doesn't even acknowledge us. He knows what troop we're from, and he hates Casper. Earlier in the week he tried to get us kicked out of the camp, on account of our conduct at Taps, but nobody did anything. They were too afraid of us. Every night the other troop stands at attention while the flag is lowered, while we put our hands in our pockets and whistle over the pathetic hooting of their fat-faced bugler. Their scoutmaster closes his eyes in fury, and when the sound dies he marches his kids quickly down the hill to his own camp.

The troop passes the stone wall and Heitman Maces the last kid in line as he marches by, eyes forward. It's quick and the kid doesn't seem to know what it is, he just wipes his neck and marches on. They tromp out of sight around the corner of the pool, the kid shaking his head, and Heitman stashes the Mace under a loose stone that has fallen from the wall. "Crap doesn't work," he says. "Wouldn't you know?" We walk the long way back to camp and Heitman traps a black rat snake next to the path. Back in the tent we put it in a box and collect tree toads. The snake swallows four toads before Heitman throws it into the hot-water tank. It boils and turns gray and hard as a spring, its eyes completely white.

The seniors are grimly practicing being Indians for the ceremony when the scoutmaster from the other troop marches in, red-faced. He walks up to Casper, his forefinger shaking, and wants to see all of the troop. One of his boys got sent to the hospital after being shot in the face with something. It might have been acid, he says. He'll know the boys who did it when he sees them. He knows they're here.

I come out of the tent in full uniform, more or less, trying to disguise myself. Heitman is nowhere to be found. Casper lines us up and the scoutmaster starts at one end, looking each of us up and down for a long time, then moving on to the next. His face is still red, and his mouth set, but after a few kids it's clear he's not cut out for this sort of thing. He's starting to lose his nerve; he's too soft. Even fat Porter senses it and seems to sneer at him. Casper follows next to him and tries to keep him moving along the line. He's on our side.

There is a noise behind me and Heitman moves in next to me, naked except for his gray underpants. He stands rigid, almost not breathing, perfectly at attention. His bony chest is thrust out and the hollows above his collarbone are so deep they're shadowed. The scoutmaster gets even with me, takes one look, and taps Casper on the shoulder. "That's one of them," he says, pointing at me. I look at Casper and his face is stone.

"Which was he," he says. "The one with the can or the other one?"

"The other one," says the scoutmaster, already moving on. He stops and squints at Heitman. He looks at Heitman's face but not at the rest of him. Heitman's face is cold, reptilian. His eyes don't blink and don't focus. The scoutmaster draws away for a second, then leans forward, close to Heitman's face. "Have you got a problem, young man, standing here in your underpants?" Heitman smiles softly, then looks the scoutmaster in the eye. Up close, the scoutmaster's face is soft and freckled, and his eyelashes are just wisps of white above his eyes. He has a sparse moustache that sticks out slightly, trying to hide a hare-lip. The moustache quivers, like a rabbit, and it is a second before I realize that it is something the scoutmaster can't con-trol. He stands there, staring at Heitman, and everyone knows after a couple of seconds he doesn't have the courage to call him out.

Sure enough, he moves on and finishes the line. Under the bus tarp the seniors have quit being Indians and sit around a table, playing cards loud and smoking cigarettes. When they notice the scoutmaster looking at them, they lower their cards and stare at him. The scoutmaster looks for a moment as if he might go over, but thinks the better of it and turns around. He sees Casper walk up to me and slap me hard across the face.

"Who was it?" Casper says. "Talk to me and I won't kick the living shit out of you."

"Hey," says the scoutmaster, "there's no need for that." I hold my face and start to cry. The scoutmaster shoves in front of Casper and bends down at the waist, his hand on my shoulder. "No one's going to hurt you," he says. He's breathing hard and his hand shakes on my shoulder. "I have a boy in the hospital," he says. "You understand?" I shake my head and my throat snags when I breathe in.

The scoutmaster turns to Casper. "I mean, he's going to be all right and everything. It's just the idea." Casper looks at him without saying anything. The scoutmaster shakes his head, his face is terrible to look at. "I mean," he says, "I mean the boy is *hurt*." He looks at all of us but nobody says a word, and after a moment he just walks off the way he came. Casper watches him go and when the scoutmaster is out of sight he sighs. He puts his hand on my shoulder but I can tell he doesn't like touching me.

"Show me the can, you stupid shit," he says, his voice almost gentle. I look up at him with gratitude, but he's not looking at me. He stands with his hand on my neck but looks at Heitman, who is still at attention, his underwear sagging in front.

"Heitman," he says, "one more time and that's it."

Casper walks me back along the path to the stone wall, and I point out the can, under its rock. He picks it up, hefts it, and puts it in his pocket. After a moment he sits down on the wall and I sit next to him. He picks up his legs and crosses them under him, his elbows on his thighs, his metal-toed boot tips tucked behind his knees.

"Heitman's crazy, you know," he says. He stares down the road where the other troop came from. "I used to never think kids could be crazy but that kid's crazy."

He looks at me like I should explain and I know I have to say something. I think of Heitman at the river in the moonlight and say the first thing I think of.

"He's got scars," I whisper.

Casper is quiet for a second. "Where?"

I tell him and he sighs softly. His shoulders sag and he closes his eyes, just for a moment.

"You know," he says, "I was thinking of tapping him out tomorrow night. I thought it might be just the thing for him."

"Maybe," I say.

His voice drops low and his face gets dreamy. "The Indians used to make their boys go out into the wilderness for months, just living off the land. When they came back they were men. That's what the Order of the Arrow ceremony is based on."

"Alone?" I say.

He looks at me sharply. "They look for their spirit guide," he says. "An animal, like an eagle or a mountain lion, to lead them. Then they become one."

I want to correct him. He doesn't know Heitman the way I do. I know what Heitman would do to any animal that tried to lead him anywhere, or become one with him. Instead I say nothing, and Casper shakes his head and looks away from me. A second later he gets up and walks back up the path to camp. I follow him, not too far behind.

When we get back to the camp Heitman is sitting with the seniors, smoking, looking pleased with himself. Casper walks up and takes his cigarette away and throws it into the cooking fire. He walks behind him and looks at his back. I know what he's looking for, and I can't remember for the life of me why I told him that. Casper shoots me a dark look and goes inside his tent and pulls the flaps shut. Chadwell hands Heitman another cigarette and Heitman lights it directly from the fire, his face nearly in the flames, impressing the hell out of the seniors. When I go to get some wood I pass close to them, and hear them invite Heitman to spend the night in their tent. He smokes his cigarette and smiles at them all, one at a time.

Sometime that night he parts the flaps to my tent. His underwear is gone. I have been awake, expecting him, lying on my back and gripping the sides of my cot. I've been expecting him because I did not hear him howl.

"Come on out, Bergman," he says. "Let's go explore."

I say nothing. I lie stiff, not moving, watching him under my eyelids. He crouches in the doorway, one knee up and the other down.

"Berrr-gie," he whispers, "Bergie, Bergie, Bergie . . ." I hold my chest tight, trying not to breathe. After a moment the tent flaps fall closed and Heitman is gone. His footsteps blend into the crickets and the bullfrogs and the sound of Old Willy's television. I lie awake and listen for him but he doesn't come back.

When I wake up Friday morning Heitman is still gone. Disappeared. He is still missing at breakfast. By lunch Casper is cussing and Old Willy is passing out trail maps to the seniors. Chadwell tosses his in the breakfast fire and laughs, but stops when Casper sticks another one in his chest. "Find him," he says, "or don't come back." He snatches the feathers from Chadwell's hair. "And get that shit out of here."

The seniors take me with them, almost running down the trail. A quarter mile from camp they stop as if on a signal and sit on some rocks, begin smoking cigarettes. Garcia offers me one of my own but I say no. After about ten minutes they set off again, slower, and tromp as much around the path as on it. Nobody makes any effort to call out Heitman's name, or look away from the path. Chadwell walks along breaking off branches and Garcia strips leaves from everything he touches. What did you dare him to do this time, I wonder. Did you send him off into the wilderness alone, looking for himself as a man? Their backs don't answer me, and we walk on and on.

Two hours later we're back, running the last few hundred yards into the camp. It is abandoned except for Old Willy, who is asleep under the TV tarp. When Casper returns with a ranger he is rigid with anger; throughout dinner he is dead silent. Some whisper that the seniors took Heitman out into the woods during the night and abandoned him; others think he just ran away. By nightfall it becomes possible to believe the boy is dead. We wait in our tents for the call to the Indian ceremony; I leave the flap open for Heitman but he doesn't come.

The woods are black beyond the light thrown by the line of torches. There is no moon and the wind makes the trees brush up against each other in waves. Our line marches down the side of a ravine. The path is pebbly and some of the boys slip, reaching out to the man in front, sometimes bringing them both down. On the ground they are kicked by the Indians until they get up. If they try to brush their clothes they are struck on the shoulders with wooden lances. Porter starts to cry and two Indians whisk him out of line. Nobody turns to see what happens to him.

At the end of the path, at the bottom of the ravine, is a bonfire and in front of it stands a lone Indian, his arms folded. It is obviously Casper, in leather pants and striped makeup. In the light of the fire his tattoos seem to dance up one arm and down the other. His eyes are closed. We line up in front of him and the bonfire. The other troop is lined up on the far side of the fire, standing quietly. Unlike us they are in full uniform—their scoutmaster is also in uniform, and stands to the right of them. They blink and their eyes shift; one of them raises a hand to wipe his nose. I expect an Indian to rush up and knock the boy to the ground, but nothing happens. Suddenly my head is grabbed from behind and jerked side to

39

side. "Eyes front," someone hisses in my ear. I smell cigarettes; I know it's Garcia, and I stand as still as I can.

Casper opens his eyes. He picks up a feathered pole and walks the line of the other troop. He stops and shakes the pole in front of a boy, and one of the other Indians steps up and taps the boy on the chest with his flattened hand, once, then twice. The boy steps forward and the Indian leads him up to the fire, hands him an arrow. The boy's face is cold and he stands with his arms folded, facing his old friends across the clearing, the arrow held diagonally across his chest.

Casper has two more boys tapped from the other troop, then starts with us, at the far side from me. My heart begins throbbing and my body starts to itch, but I can hear the crunch of footsteps behind me, and I can smell Garcia as he passes. I feel my pulse in my fingertips and in my shrunken stomach and I want to race back to camp where Old Willy is running the generator and watching television. I listen to the progress of Garcia from one end and Casper from the other, one in back and the other in front.

Casper shakes his pole and one of our own is tapped out, one of the older boys. The Indian hits him hard in the chest, much harder than the other troop, but he is ready, one foot slightly back, and the sound of flesh on flesh is so loud it echoes off the trees around us. The troop across the clearing sways in line at the sound, their eyes widening. Our boy walks forward and stands in front of us, his back to the fire. He stares over our heads.

Casper taps out one more, then two. He moves down the

line and then stops dead in front of me. My heart clenches in my chest and my breath starts to catch in my throat. I am sure he sees me crying. He looks me in the eye and his face is too dark to see clearly, but I can see his eyes. They look crazy; the moisture in them reflects the beating of the bonfire. He stands there, staring at me, his chest rising and falling. He seems to stand there forever. Please, I say to myself, please. I want you to. Then he smiles, but in a bad way, the way Heitman smiles at fat Porter. I close my hot eyes when his feet crunch away from me.

He reaches the end of the line without again shaking the pole. The Indian behind him takes his place next to the three boys, and Casper walks to the bonfire and turns to face the rest of us—the small ones, the ones left over. He raises his arms high up from his sides, eyes squeezed nearly shut, and his chest starts to swell, getting ready to shout at the treetops. Because he is like this, he doesn't see Heitman walk slowly into the light of the clearing. When he opens his eyes and sees him, whatever he was thinking of shouting comes out instead as a kind of twisted yelp. His arms fall to his sides like shot birds.

Heitman is naked, smeared with mud in streaks across his sides. There is blood on his legs and what looks like shit in his hair. He carries something in his arms; a big mess of blood and bone and feathers sticking out this way and that. He is naked, but he walks with his skinny shoulders back, up on the balls of his feet. The way he moves makes the Indians look like schoolkids lost in the woods in their pajamas. They stare at him—next to them one of the chosen boys drops his arrow in

41

the dirt. Casper, like a deflating balloon, sits down right where he was standing.

Heitman has caught a wild turkey, and killed it. Heitman has caught a wild turkey with his bare hands. He doesn't say anything, he just stands and faces us, the turkey in his arms. He looks exhausted; he looks done in. We glance at each other and we start to move and shuffle in our places, and just then fat Porter goes and does it. He starts in and after a second everybody joins him. We stand there, the small ones, all in a line in front of Heitman and the bonfire and the Indians, and we howl. We howl and we howl, and Heitman smiles down the line at us all, one at a time. When he gets to me his eyes rest only for a second, then drift on past to the next boy. My heart clenches again, but it is too late; now we are all Heitman's girlfriend.

le-
s**a**bre

t is late afternoon, late fall, and the office is quiet for a Friday. In my cubicle there is only me and my phone, me and my CRT, me and my adding machine and coffee cup. The buzzing in my telephone receiver doesn't carry very far—at about six or seven inches it is as if the line were dead. But it isn't dead. There's a woman on the other end reaching that point of hysteria possible only late on a Friday. Unfortunately, there is nothing I can do for her. She isn't covered; she didn't make her payments and her policy has lapsed. It's my job to explain to her that if she drives, she does so at her own risk, that she has no protection, that if anything happens, it happens. There is nothing I can do for her unless she pays her premium.

"But, you see, I'll have the money in two days, just a couple of days. My boy in Pittsburgh mailed the check, I talked to him today and he said he put it in the mail." She sounds out of breath.

"Ma'am. Mrs. Williams. Please listen to me carefully. If we get your check within ten days of the cancellation date, which was only yesterday, then we can reinstate you without a lapse in coverage. Do you see?"

"Yes, sir, I see that, sir, but I still don't understand. I

thought you said I was cancelled, now you tell me I have ten days."

"I'm sorry. It's my fault. I'm confusing you." I take a deep breath. "At this moment you *are* cancelled, officially, as of yesterday at midnight, and you will remain cancelled until we receive your check. If we receive it before ten days from yesterday, the thirteenth, then, and only then, I can go *back* to yesterday at midnight on my computer and reinstate your policy in full, as if no break had ever occurred."

"So what you're saying is that if I pay you day after tomorrow then I won't be cancelled yesterday. Am I right, sir?"

"Yes, uh, that's right. Is that clear for you, Mrs. Williams?" There is something wrong with her understanding of the situation, I'm sure. She has rattled me a little, and the hand I'm holding the phone with is sweaty.

"I think so. I think I see. What you're saying is that if I go out tonight and get myself in a wreck, and then pay you day after tomorrow, you folks will still pay me for my car?"

"Well, technically, yes."

"And you'll pay for my hospital, too?"

"We'll cover everything that you have on your policy."

"So then I'm covered to go to work tonight, am I right?"

Oh, Jesus Christ. "No, Mrs. Williams, *no.* You are cancelled until we get the money. I can do absolutely nothing until I get a check—that's how it works. How can I make you understand that?" Even as I ask her I realize there is no way. No way to add to the already shaky idea of insurance the extra dimension of retroactivity, that you can affect tomorrow what happened yesterday, or the day after tomorrow the day before that. What Mrs. Williams is hearing is exactly what she wants to hear, what she needs to hear, that someone is there for her *now*, not contingent on some future event, or check. Her voice rises in pitch.

"But you tell me I'll be clean when I pay you, I'll never have been cancelled at all, and never includes today and I'm going to pay you tomorrow, so why do you tell me I'm cancelled when I'm not? How can you tell me that? How?"

God, I'm lost—I'm so bad at dealing with this kind of thing. "Because tomorrow hasn't come, Mrs. Williams. You're cancelled. If you drive today it will be without insurance. If you kill or maim someone, *you* are responsible, not me. If you wreck your car, then you'll have to walk. If someone hits you and sends you to the hospital, then you'll have to get a lawyer and sue him because I won't help you. I *can't*, Mrs. Williams. I'd like to, I'd give the world to, but I simply can't. Do you understand?"

"No." She is crying. "I don't understand. First you tell me that I'm covered, then you tell me I'm not. Are you my insurance man or not? Are you going to protect me or not? I can't drive without insurance. I don't want to kill anybody, I just want to go to work." I hear a few gulps of static. "And then maybe just a little trip to the store. I won't even leave town, I won't leave the city. What could happen, mister sir, what could happen?"

"Mrs. Williams, I . . ."

"I *need* to use my car, I *need* it."

"Mrs. . . ."

"Can I please go to work, sir?"

The phone is slippery in my hand. The breathing I hear in the receiver is my own. I hate things like this, I hate them.

"Okay, Mrs. Williams, okay." I put the receiver down on the desk, breathe a deep breath, and then pick it back up. "Mrs. Williams, I'll extend your policy for one week, but one week only. Your new expiration date is one week from yesterday. Go to work, Mrs. Williams."

She piles on the gratitude: God bless you, you won't be sorry, I'll be careful. To her I am protection; in her mind I can offer her another week of security just by stating so. I wonder what she thinks I'll do, push a paper, make a new line on my CRT? It makes no difference that I really can't do a thing to stop some city bus from making a sorry turn and crushing her into her Pinto, that I can't gently take that last drink from her hand and drive her home, can't yank the kid on the skateboard out of her unconscious way. What's ludicrous is that I can't do even what I promised her I would. I can no more change the expiration date of a policy than I could be God. If she gets into an accident she will call the office and whoever answers will refer her to Claims. Claims will look at their screen and tell her that they're sorry, but she wasn't covered at the time of the accident. She will tell them that the nice man on the phone fixed everything and told her she was covered until the check arrived. They will politely ask her the name of the nice man, they will still deny the claim, and then

I will be out of work again, and Mrs. Williams will be out of luck.

ow Cal's wife Gloria is on the phone. Cal is my supervisor and an old friend from college. Cal and I go out drinking on Friday nights with Fred from across the hall, and Gloria is calling me because she is worried about tonight. It's strange. She has never called me before; I barely know her. I'd met her ten years ago at a frat party in school, and then once again a few days after I started with the company. Both times she treated me as if I were a great deal younger than she was, and both times she called me by the wrong name. She knows it well enough now, though.

"Christopher, as long as *you* drive. Will you promise me that *you* will drive? Will you promise me that?"

"Gloria, I always drive, you know that."

"I know, I know, but tonight I feel more worried than usual, or something. I don't know. I'm afraid something's going to happen. Will you just humor me, please?"

"I promise I'll drive."

"You know, why don't you guys go bowling or something on Fridays? All the guys in my office go bowling on Fridays. Cal can bowl, I've seen him, he's very good, and he looked like he was having fun. Why don't you guys do that?"

I look over at Cal. He's been listening in on the extension and he makes horrible grimacing faces when she mentions bowling. I try to look away from him but he doesn't want me to, and he tries actively to keep my eye.

"You know, Gloria, that's a good idea. I could get into bowling tonight. I think we will go bowling, that should be fun." Cal sticks two fingers down his throat and makes silent vomiting motions. I frown at him, and he laughs silently with his shoulders.

"You know, Chris, I don't know what I'd do without you. I think I'd worry myself to death or something. Cal is really insufferable when the winter starts to set in—he goes stir-crazy or something."

Cal rolls his eyes back into his head and I look away. "Don't worry about it, Gloria. I don't mind driving, and I have the most room in my car, anyway."

"Oh, I know all that. I just like the thought of you driving better. You know, in case anything happens and all. Oh, and, Chris?"

"Yes?"

"Please don't be afraid to call me."

"Call you?"

"You know, if anything happens."

"Okay, Gloria. If anything happens."

"Oh, Chris, thanks a bunch. I feel much better. You guys have fun tonight. Bye."

Cal hangs up his phone a second after I do, then leans forward and puts his elbows on his desk. I'm a little rattled, but I get up and go over to his desk. He is the area supervisor, and his desk is at the inside point of a fan of cubicles, facing our backs.

"Chris, the Bandit says he can't go out tonight." The Bandit is Fred from Life and Health, the office across the hall. Cal christened him the Bandit because he chews Bandit tobacco ever since he quit smoking. Actually, he looks very little like a Bandit and very much like the insurance salesman he is. He is a short, soft man with skin that looks like damp wax fruit. Cal is always riding him about chewing those little paper pouches of tobacco. Fred says they keep his teeth from getting discolored. Cal says they're like trying to suck tit through a sweater.

"Why can't he go out?" I run my hand through my hair, still thinking about Gloria and Mrs. Williams.

"I don't know—why don't you talk to him?" Cal picks up his phone, punches a few buttons. "Bandit, get over here, you prick of misery." He hangs up the phone and in a moment Fred appears in the doorway—Cal is technically his boss as well—and stops there. "Bandit, Chris is pissed that you're not going tonight. Tell him why."

"I can't afford it, Cal. I really can't."

"What's to afford? Chris already said he was driving, we'll pick up some beers and drink those in the car, and Chris and I'll pick up your tab at Jonathan's, you cheap bastard. What's to afford?" Cal suddenly smiles, his eyebrows high, as if he'd just sold the Bandit a car.

Fred looks uneasily at me, then back at Cal.

Cal spreads his hands. "What do you say, Bandit? Is it a bender?"

The Bandit nods. "Okay, but not too late. I got to get up in the morning."

Cal snorts. "What have you got to do in the morning, you prick of misery?"

"I got to do yard work."

"Have your goddamn wife mow the lawn. You're not pulling in till noon tomorrow, cowboy." Cal pulls his tie from his collar, throws it into a drawer in his credenza, and slams it shut. "No, sir. You are in it for the duration, Bandit." He takes a few papers from his desk and puts them in his PENDING basket. He stops. "You are two very lucky guys. We're gonna have a good one tonight." He scoots his chair back and takes his suit coat off the back of it. "All right then, we're out of here."

We are already in the elevator when I realize that I left my coat and keys and wallet at my desk, my terminal still signed on, and my phone on READY.

n Chicago's northwest suburbs, around O'Hare, everything is low-slung and trendy, new to the point of staleness. There are very few trees or tall buildings to blot out the sky, and on clear nights you can see twenty, sometimes thirty landing lights hanging in the atmosphere as if they had been strung together along enormous wires. Some circle, others seem to hover, still others recede like comets that had come too close to the sun and were hurled away. None ever seems to touch the ground.

We leave Cal's and Fred's cars in the parking garage and take my Buick LeSabre. It used to be Cal's. He sold it to me when I moved back to the suburbs from the East flat-broke and took the job he'd dug up for me. It's the car we always take, ostensibly because it's roomy, but really because I always drive. It seems to have worked out that way, but I don't mind. The LeSabre is really a good car.

Cal sits in the passenger seat up front—shotgun, he called it in college, and still does—and plays with the radio endlessly, adjusting the tone and the faulty balance control. I watch him out of the side of my eye as I drive. Cal has a strange kind of adolescent attractiveness that has skated him easily through his thirty years. He is a big man. His face is open, slightly red and blustery, and good-looking in a way that made women in college want to go home with him and men include him in on their team, or on their side of an argument. He married Gloria without telling anyone, the week after graduation, and the next day they moved to the suburbs of Chicago where her folks lived. We never saw them pack or anything. For some reason, I've always felt that I could only be friends with one of them, and Cal has never invited me to his home.

Fred opens beers in the backseat, handing one forward to each of us. I take it and put it between my legs. There is little to do until dark. Fred and Cal talk about insurance, about someday opening their own agency. That is where the real

53

money is in insurance, not at the corporate level. Fred used to teach high school but quit because the money was no good and he got no respect from his students. He is nervous about drinking in the car, and watches from the backseat like a teenager. He makes a pretty unexciting Bandit.

Cal is getting more and more animated talking about his future agency. "We can get a book of business from the rejects at work right now. I got access to all that information— names, addresses. We'll take the best of them, the ones that just barely didn't qualify, and charge them out the bummy- hole. They're no worse risk than anyone else, and the best thing is, they got no place else to go."

Fred seems unconvinced. He knows the move is illegal as hell, but also that there was very little chance that they would ever get caught. "I don't know, Cal. Anything can happen with those guys. We don't know what's been on their record and dropped after a couple of years. I think we should get the old folks. Get them on the books with a lowball quote and hang on to them. They're the best risk, the best return, if you ask me."

Cal's face is getting red. "Bandit? What are you, *kidding*? A hundred fucking dollars a year when we can get a *thousand*? Fifteen *hundred*? Just what do you think these guys are going to do?"

"I don't know, Cal. It just sounds like we'd be making money off other people's misfortune."

"So?" Cal raises his hands and lets them drop. "So what do you want? Where you been? We can't lead their fucking lives

54

for them. It's gonna happen, let it happen, for Christ's sake. We provide a service they're gonna *need*, so there's no reason we can't make a buck off it."

The Bandit shakes his head but doesn't answer. Cal stares at him for a few seconds and then turns back around to the front. Nobody speaks. We are on a side road, running parallel to a highway, where the few surrounding fields have managed to stay cultivated amid the foaming growth of the suburbs around them. Up ahead of us, walking along the gravel shoulder, is a boy of about thirteen, and ahead of him is a smaller boy, about a hundred feet further up. The first boy turns and watches us approach, and he grips something in his fist, away from the road.

Cal touches me on the shoulder with his free hand. "Chris, watch this goddamn kid, he's gonna throw something at the car."

We come up nearer to the kid and he turns toward us, walking backward, and he looks at the car with a blank expression. It is dusk, but my lights aren't on yet and I can't make out what is in his hand. It could be rocks or dried corn from the small field next to him. I slow down a little, but not enough to make him notice any difference.

Cal touches me again, leaning over to my side. "Get ready to lock up the brakes if the little fucker throws anything." His voice sounds excited; whether it is from the conversation with Fred or from the kid, I can't tell.

I watch the kid through the windshield as we approach, and after we pass I turn my eyes up to the rearview to see if

55

he has done anything. He has turned with the car, and in an instant I see a look of shock go over his face.

Cal screams. "Jesus!" I turn ahead and see the other boy has drifted out into the road and in front of the car. I stamp on the brakes and the LeSabre screams and throws us forward. The little boy turns as the car bears down on him, his knees buckle, his face draws back, and he puts his hands out in front of him—palms forward, as if holding off a blow. Just when it looks like we will stop in time, the car goes through him and he goes up onto the hood on his stomach. The tires grab the road completely, the LeSabre locks onto the ground, and the boy slides off, disappearing below the hood.

We rock slightly, frozen for a moment, and then I jump out of the car and run to the kid. He's sitting back on the road about five feet in front of the grill with his hands behind him, his face contorted, twitching. As I reach him he jumps to his feet, staring at me for three seconds, four, his face asking me how he should feel. He starts to blink and sniffle.

"Are you all right?" I put my hands on his shoulders, and he wrenches them away. "Wait a minute, now, wait a minute. Come here." The words spill out of my mouth as if they were still in the car, flying forward. "Sit down or something, you might be hurt. Are you all right or what?" He lurches away from me, and then the older boy comes running around the car and takes him by the shoulders the same way I did. The smaller kid tries to wrap himself around the larger boy, but he holds him firmly away, leans down to his ear, and speaks into it.

"Are you all right?" The little boy wiggles in his grasp but doesn't answer. As the big kid runs his hands around him, checking him, the little boy finally bursts into tears. The older one holds the boy and looks up at me, his face startlingly passive, and he shakes his head. "He's only scared. He always cries when he's scared."

I walk a step closer to them. "Are you sure he's all right?"

"Oh, yeah. He's just scared. He must not've seen you, and he hasn't got his hearing aid in 'cause we've been swimming at school. He's my little brother." He says this as if this was a disclaimer of some kind. "I'm really sorry."

"But I hit him with the car. He might have broken ribs or something. Ask him if he hurt his ribs. Make him breathe in and out."

He leans his head down and speaks into the boy's ear. The little boy shakes his head violently and continues crying. I hear a noise and look beside me. Cal is standing there, looking very calm. Everyone is so fucking calm but me, I'm still shaking.

Cal walks up to me and whispers in my ear. "It's all right. I took care of it." I nod without really listening. The small one has started to let up on his crying, and his brother pushes him gently away and looks up at us.

"It's all right, sir, okay?" He smiles and I feel a little faint. He starts walking away and the little boy waits a moment, then runs up and grabs onto the back of his shirt. The older boy turns back to us and shrugs, embarrassed. "It's okay, really." They walk off down the dark road, the little boy still sniffling.

Without looking at Cal or Fred, I walk back to the car. In the dust, high on the hood, are two handprints that pull down to a large smudge surrounding the LeSabre insignia. I stare at it a long moment before walking around to my door.

When I get in the car, I'm almost surprised to find Cal sitting next to me. He is opening another beer. "Cal, what did you mean when you said you took care of it?"

He looks at me like I was a slow child. "The beers."

I shake my head slowly, confused, then look down at my seat. It is wet, and there is a stain on my trousers. My can is not in sight.

"I took care of it." Cal grins, eyebrows high, and opens another can, handing it to me. "You better turn around and go the other way, cowboy. Just to be on the safe side."

I do it without thinking.

There are a lot of people at Jonathan's, but a couple of spots are free at the bar and Cal and I grab them. Fred stands behind us and tries to keep out of the waitress's way. I feel like drinking. The accident seems to have jarred something loose inside of me, something that flutters in my throat and down into my stomach. Something that makes me feel like I should be seeing something behind me, or around me. I don't know if Fred or Cal feels anything. The three of us are silent.

The beers arrive and they seem light, the glasses small. The bartenders, both young, work quickly, always seeming to be blending something or shaking something else. They are quiet in the noisy atmosphere around them, and take orders with raised eyebrows, as if they had been tapped on the shoulder, while making no less than two drinks at a time. Jonathan's is across from the airport, a young kind of crowd, and although we have been coming here almost every Friday for the two months since Cal hired me, I get no hint of recognition from the bartenders. I take my change without a word, my hand still shaking.

After a few moments, Cal gets up and wanders off, and Fred follows. I stay with my beer and look at myself in the mirrored tiles behind the bar. I can see a dozen or so fractured reflections of myself, looking more like an insurance man than I had ever thought possible—the receding hairline, the sour expression of undigestible lunches, as if my tongue had swollen against my mouth, the guilty stare. I'd known when I started that I wouldn't last as an insurance man; it was just a question of how soon I would quit, or how quickly I'd be fired. I'd pictured a quiet job filling in forms, draping my only suit coat lazily over the back of my chair, sipping coffee. Instead I find myself working for an old friend I don't know anymore, following instructions in a language I don't quite understand—and every Friday doing roughly the same thing in a bar. It turns out there are no forms, nothing nearly that concrete—only delicately flashing green figures, and phone conversations with people whose only contact with me will involve money or disaster. I'm not in control; I am miles behind.

As I think this, something comes to me, striking me with

a force that makes my head bob. I look back up at myself in the mirror. Insurance, the whole idea of it as protection, is a lie. Insurance is just a big brother, a slightly embarrassed brother who runs up to you after something hits you, then dusts you off, feels for bruises, apologizes to the other guy, and walks you a little way down the road.

In the darkness behind me the dance-floor lights sparkle and swing. I can't look at myself in the mirrors without seeing those lights as well, so I turn and watch the people move around. Fred is on the dance floor with a pretty woman, young, who dances without looking at him. As I watch, the song changes into another without stopping and the woman walks away from the floor. Fred follows her and stands next to her table, looking over his raised glass back at the dance floor as she ignores him, leaning over closer to someone at the table.

I suddenly feel the need to talk to someone, someone important, someone detached from all this, and I remember what Gloria had said on the phone. I walk to the entryway, to the pay phone in front of the hostess stand, and I put a quarter in. I dial and the line clicks, then buzzes busy. I hang up and walk back to the bar.

In the corner near the back I can see Cal seated across a small table from a woman who seems to be absorbed in whatever he is saying. I look away, over toward my seat at the bar, and then back to them. They are both laughing. From where I am, I can't make out what the woman looks like, but she

60

seems small, young, like the girls who work at car-rental counters. She holds her drink up next to her face, her elbow on the table, while Cal talks with both his hands on the table as if he were trying to show her with body language that he is an up-front and honest individual.

I go to the bar, pick up my glass, and walk over to their table. As I get closer I can see that the woman is dressed very casually, with a dark jacket and small boots, and her sleeves are folded back to show bracelets, at least five on each arm, that have slid down below her cuffs. Her lips are bright red and her drink is equally red. She is older than I had thought, at least as old as Cal.

Cal looks up and waves me into a chair, an annoyed smile on his face. "Tina, this is Chris, my roommate. Chris, Tina."

My roommate. Cal has tried this once before, and although he didn't get the woman home, I had gone along with the whole thing. I smile at her and put my glass on the table. "Hello, Tina. How are you?"

"I am fine." She says this quite slow and I realize that she is mimicking my tone, the note of profound knowledge and pity that I can't keep from my voice. It's quite possible she does not want me there. I look her in the eye and she turns away from me, back to Cal.

Cal touches me on the shoulder. "Tina's a broker from Hartford. Property and Casualty."

She nods. "Personal Lines, actually." She gives Cal a meaningful look, but it is lost on him.

I clear my throat. "Tina." She looks back at me, her eyebrows raised, somewhat patronizing. "So what do you think of my roommate? Isn't he fascinating?"

She taps her glass. "I don't know. I really haven't had much of a chance to find out. He was just now telling me about your apartment." She is so damn snippy, it slows me. It is as if she is at cruising speed and I am an annoying billboard, a static-filled radio.

"Oh, yes. Our apartment. It's really great. Really too small for two grown men, but we get by." I feel something creep into my voice, something wise and sly. Cal smiles pointedly at me, his brain squirming, I'm sure, and I imagine him trying to kick me under the table. I smile back at him. "I was just lucky that my brother was good enough to let me move in."

The woman looks surprised, and she drops her arrogance. "You two are brothers?" She looks at Cal. "You didn't tell me that." Cal says nothing.

"Oh, yes." I pat Cal on the shoulder. "We're twins. Fraternal. Siamese, actually."

"What?" Her eyes narrow. She has a kind of a smirk on her face now, not really a smile.

"That's right. I was born with Cal sticking out of my chest, right above my heart, kicking me in the face. My wife Gloria says the scar on my chest looks like a bowling ball." At the mention of her name, Cal's face goes a little pale.

Tina's smirk widens. "All right, I'll play." She opens her small bag and takes out a cigarette. She taps it on the table and looks at Cal, then at me. "Why are you living in his apartment if you're married?" She lights the cigarette and blows the smoke downward, toward my drink, looking at me expectantly.

"Tina, how do you know that I'm married? I could be lying. I could just be playing some kind of game with you."

She frowns. "Well, you're drunk, I know that."

"Nope. Not tonight. I promised Gloria no drinking, or was it no driving?" I look at Cal. "I can't remember." His face has gone red, but he is silent. He's wondering if I intend to salvage this thing for him. "Tell her, Cal. Tell her that I'm really married and that I just use your place to take unsuspecting women. Tell her that my wife sits at home every night while I go out and play the field and get drunk and pretend to have fun. No, really, go ahead and tell her, Cal."

Cal looks me hard in the eye. It fuels me. I hold my finger up in front of him and swing my head back to the woman. "Are you covered?"

She narrows her eyes, no longer smiling. "What are you talking about now?"

"It's a simple question. Are you covered?"

She shakes her head. "Are you talking about insurance? What are you talking about?"

"I assume you have a car, and I'm sure it's insured. You probably rent, or maybe own a condo, so you have renter's or homeowner's. Am I right so far?"

"I don't believe this." She puts her cigarette down. "You're not about to try and sell me . . ."

"I'm not going to try and sell you anything, Tina. Tonight it's free. You've heard of life insurance?"

"Of course. What are you doing?" Her voice has changed, she is suspicious and defensive.

"You see, Tina, there's no such thing as life insurance. You've heard of fire insurance? It *causes* fires—never prevented a single one of them."

"What are you . . ."

"Come *on*, Tina. You're a professional. You're in the *business* for Christ's sake. Open your eyes."

Her lips tighten. "I still don't . . ." She stops and looks to Cal, as if for help. Cal meets her eye for only a second, then gets to his feet and walks away from the table. She stares at him for a moment, and her lips slacken, and her jaw relaxes. She looks back at me, her face finally open. Her shoulders drop a little and she puts both hands on her glass, looking down at the table. She shakes her head slowly, just barely. "I'm a big girl, you know." She breathes in and out. "I can take care of myself."

My throat grabs. "Tina." I reach for her hand but she pulls it away. "Tina, for God's sake, look around you. Look at us. We're all big." I think about this as I say it, as if I'd heard it from someone else. Suddenly I realize what I had thought wasn't about insurance at all. It was about something else, something in Tina's face, in Gloria's voice, in the Bandit's pathetic look across the dance floor.

I pull my hand back slowly and try to look into Tina's eyes, but she grinds her cigarette into the ashtray and looks over her shoulder. Her face has turned a little pale, a little humiliated. When she looks back, something comes over her like a chilled wind. Her face hardens with anger—anger at me, as if she'd been slapped. She straightens up in her chair and lets her bracelets fall to her wrists. She gets to her feet, grabbing her purse with both hands, and strides toward the restrooms with jerky, stiff steps.

I stay in my seat, feeling as if the look on her face has hurtled me to another jarring stop. I look for the Bandit but I can't find him on the floor anywhere. I stand up, a little shaky, and I walk over to the pay phone. Whatever I had glimpsed is trembling in my grasp, trying to slide away, and I am afraid to lose it. I put in a quarter and dial Cal and Gloria's number again. On the second ring the phone is picked up.

"Hello?" She waits and I can hear her breath. "Hello?" Her voice is different from what I expected, flat and lifeless. I open my mouth but there is nothing to say. I take the receiver away from my ear and look at it, as if I were trying to identify it. Another hello sounds weakly through the earpiece before the connection is broken. I keep looking at the receiver until the dial tone starts. I can't for the life of me figure out what it was I had wanted to say.

I hang up and walk out the door. Outside it's windy and cold, and the sky hangs low, lit a sickly yellow by the amber streetlights. Across the parking lot Fred the Bandit is leaning against the hood of the LeSabre holding his coat around his body, watching the door. I walk up to him.

He smiles at me, his face puffy with the cold. "I'm supposed to meet this woman out here." He tilts his head and eyes me carefully. "How are you doing?"

"Are there any jobs teaching school, Bandit?"

"Why, you quitting already?"

"Something like that." I lean up against the Buick next to him, looking up at the sky. "You know, Fred, I had this woman today who was cancelled for nonpayment, and I told her I would extend her policy for a week, just like that. No money, no check, no nothing."

Out of the corner of my eye I see Fred shrug. "So?"

"What do you mean, *so?*"

"So, I do that all the time."

I turn and look at him. "What?"

"Sure. Just fill out a red routing slip, have Cal initial it, and send it to Data Entry. I do it all the time."

"But he can't . . ."

"Yeah, I know, so don't tell anybody. He could get in trouble."

I look at Fred, incredulous, and he drips some spit between his feet and gazes back to the front door of the bar. I follow his eyes. A young, pretty couple emerges from the doorway, laughing and clutching at each other. They walk in front of us across the parking lot, pausing intermittently to look for where they left their car.

burning
luv

The cowboy hadn't even said good-bye, he just took off while I was under the bridge taking a leak. He got out just long enough to toss my backpack out onto the shoulder and then he was gone, just like that. I walked back and picked it up, a little lightheaded from the beer and reefer we'd been putting away, and wondered why he had dumped me like that. We had been talking nonstop, and the silence that fell after his little white truck crested the far hilltop seemed too hollow for an outdoors type of quiet. It felt like the quiet you might hear inside a bathroom, late at night in a bus station. It was a quiet that hurt, the way dying alone in the snow might hurt. Except that here it was hot and I was high and my pack seemed heavier than it had been before. It all of a sudden seemed a dead weight, and I was tempted to just dump it, the way the cowboy had dumped me, in the desert by the side of the interstate. I didn't, though, after all; I hefted it and tried to figure my situation.

There was some traffic coming from the east but nothing in my direction. The interstate was new and black, as if it had just spilled from the back of the truck and hadn't had time to bleach out and dust over. I-70 through Utah and west

69

Colorado was like that—most of the truckers avoided it, went north on 80 if they were heading to San Francisco or south on 40 to L.A. Nobody much used this stretch, and I was wondering, my head a little light, if I'd be sleeping outside that night. There were some mesas off the roadway that looked close enough to walk to, if a little snakey. A fire on the far side wouldn't attract attention; I'd done it before. But I didn't like the desert, and I knew I didn't want to wake up still in it.

Lately I'd been having dreams about walking through the desert. There were dead fish and busted-spine wooden boats all around me as I walked, one or two of the fish still flipping around. Snails as big as cats slipped along, looking for shade, and the ground was covered with clumps of soggy, flat-leaved amber weeds, drying to a high stink. Somewhere I had heard that the desert used to be all underwater, a gigantic sea bigger than all the oceans put together, cruised by dinosaur fish and eels the size of tankers. But out in the real desert there were no puddles, no mud, nothing but dirt and small, flat stones. The air dried out the inside of your nose, cracked your lips and made your spit taste alkaline. Here and there was a lizard, or a roly-poly bug, but they weren't much for company. Any birds you saw flew in high arcs, horizon to horizon; they might have been jets.

Along about an hour came a guy in a Jeep. He pulled it over and I liked the fact he had a gas tank strapped to the back, so right off I showed him my nine-millimeter and marched him out about a mile into the desert, bouncing along behind him in the Jeep. I was feeling easy still from the grass so I didn't let him think he had anything to worry about, bulletwise. I even let him keep his Thermos, although it only had coffee in it, and found him a Mars bar from a paper bag on the floor. I told him how it all worked, how if he prayed for me he could probably find his wheels in Grand Junction or even Denver if I felt adventurous. He prayed—they always pray when they think they're getting their machine back as part of the deal—and I left him there on his knees, with a piece of advice about rattlesnakes and hitchhikers: Don't pick either of them up.

The Jeep was one of those older ones that tended to flip, so I strapped myself in and flipped it. It had a roll bar but I still managed to put a crack in the windshield, a nice arc across the driver's side corner. The Jeep ended up on its side and I had to unstrap myself and drop to the ground, then shove the thing over. Right off the bat I was sorry. The gas tank had been flung off the back and ruptured; a bad omen. I kicked the side of the Jeep and cursed myself. It was a good idea to avoid getting gas in other people's cars, especially if they're hard-borrowed. Gas in a can was a blessing, and I had ruined it. Those Jeeps get maybe fifteen on a good day.

I got back out on the interstate about the time I started to come down. My stomach was rising up on me, empty and hot, and my head hurt with the wind slapping around my ears. The sun was dead behind me, nearly down, setting off the scenery with bands of orange. The sky was the burnt blue color of a rifle barrel. I began to hate the cowboy hard for what he did to me, and brought the Jeep up to eighty. He had a good lead but his little Jap pickup wasn't good for more than fifty-five.

We'd gotten together in the basement of a VFW in Salt Lake. A Brigham Young football game was on the TV and we were both bad-mouthing the home team from different ends of the bar. In the whole place there was only a short necker-chiefed barmaid and between us at the bar a couple of old purplenoses with windbreakers and watery eyes talking with hunched backs about their problems with the VA.

"Now how about *that* fatass," the cowboy was saying, pointing up at the TV. "Goddamn Mormons ought to just stay out of sports altogether, if you ask me."

The barmaid glowered at him. "Hey, there, language," she said. She looked at me like I was the type to agree with her.

He ignored her and yelled at the TV. "Hey, that's a ball, not a Bible, you great big stupid shit." He was a tall, thin guy with a strange, happy face and a moustache that trailed down to the corners of his chin. He had a ponytail. He was smoking cigarettes that he bought one at a time from the barmaid, blowing the smoke into the top of his glass before he drank.

They showed a cheerleader right then and he took off his cowboy hat and slammed it against the stool next to him. "Hooee," he said, "like to bite her on the ass, get lockjaw, and have her drag me to death."

"Hey," said the barmaid. "Language, I said."

I pounded my fist on the bar. "No shit, buddy. Watch your fuckin' mouth."

She pointed a thick finger to the wall. "I got a phone, you know."

Then she walked over to me, smiling hard and unfriendly.

"Son," she said, "we don't want no trouble. Can you maybe get your friend to settle down some?"

I looked over at the two purplenoses and they looked into their beer glasses quick. "Which one, Mom?" I asked.

Her lips pulled back over her teeth. "I got a phone," she said again. And just like that a couple of highway troopers wandered down the stairs and the barmaid's face went all smug and hateful.

"*Boyyyys,*" she said.

The cowboy and I sort of stretched and pulled ourselves off the bar stools. On the way up the stairs he reached into a slit in the collar of his coat and pulled out a middle-sized black switchblade. Outside while I fished my pack from the bushes where I'd hid it, he stuck the knife in the tire of the patrol car, easy as you please, and it spit out steam quick like a cough. We hopped in his little Jap pickup and left with the lights out, heading southeast toward mine country, laughing and carrying on the whole way about bars and cops and Mormons in general. On the whole it was a fine time, finer than I'd had in a long time.

After a few miles of this and that, I noticed on the seat next to me sat a leather satchel, the throat wide open, and the inside was full of round, flat tins of makeup and a bright red wig. I pulled out the wig and held it up around my fist.

"What kind of cowboy wears a wig?"

"The clown kind," he said. "When I can't get a ride I clown." I looked at him blank and he took the wig from my hand. "Rodeo," he said, stuffing it back in the satchel. "And in the winter maybe your occasional liquor store."

We slept that night in the back of the truck, between horse blankets with his coat for a pillow. He'd had to hoist his saddle up onto the roof to make room, and after things settled down I noticed one of the stirrups was hanging down over the rear window like a noose, and if I moved my head just right, I could get the full moon to shine right through the center of it, all the way through the cab. After a while the moon was gone, up and west, and it wasn't long before the cowboy snored me to sleep, his hand on the small of my back. I slept good; it was the first night in a long time that I didn't have the desert dream.

Back when I was married, after the Navy and all that horseshit, I thought that making money was all there was to do. The way I looked at it, there wasn't much of a reason to do anything else, because it came down to money anyway. I never cared much for Lia, one way or another, but she was Filipino and didn't expect much and didn't ask many questions. Her family had given me a thousand dollars to marry her and take her to the States. After I got out of Leavenworth I brought her over. Everything went okay for awhile until one night she came at me with a kitchen knife, screaming over and over she was going to "cut off you dickey, cut off you dickey." I lit out of there and never looked back.

If not for the Dishonorable I'd have gone back to the Navy. Truth is, they barely took me the first time and I'd gone begging, let me tell you. None of that jungle shit for me. The ship they stuck me on was nothing more than a gray coconut, bobbing in the South China Sea for three months at a time— it hated me and I hated it back. I was lucky, though, I had a mate named Cecil and we got along fine. He was a rancher's kid from North Dakota, just as gentle as can be, but then he went and stabbed me in the arm when I told him about me and Lia getting married back in Manila. That night he loaded himself up with foul-weather gear and metal doodads hooked to his belt and under a full moon he hopped off the coconut, his hands above his head. The duty watch saw him; he said he slid under the waves like a butter knife into dirty dishwater. None of my mates said anything, but I got the ticket, anyway; I couldn't explain the wound on my arm. Contributing to the death of a sailor, they called it, not being able to prove the other thing. I was in Kansas in less than a month.

Later, when I was living with Lia in the trailer, I started writing those letters to Cecil. Since he was dead and I didn't want them lying around, I got the smart idea of sending them to Santa Claus, care of the North Pole. I'd heard that some-body actually read those letters, somebody at the post office or somewhere, looking for kids who say they're being beat by

75

their folks. So I just wrote to Cecil, asking him about how things were down there, underneath all the waves and coconuts. I told him about how the whole thing with Lia was just for the money, and I retold it every time, in every letter. It was one of those letters that Lia found, when she, too, came at me with a knife. Man, it's something, being stabbed. Not many people can say they've been stabbed. The worst part is the itching when it starts to heal. It invites you to tear it open, get it all infected inside. The body doesn't forgive you letting something get into it like that; it knows it'll never heal right again.

After we crawled out of the back of the truck that next morning we drove into Price and ate eggs and ketchup and coffee in a place by the side of the road. The cowboy told me about his wife, that she was part Indian, Paiute, and she had been raped by her half brothers more times than she could remember. He showed me a picture of her on a postcard. It was in black and white, grainy like it was a hundred years old, and the girl in the picture looked about thirteen. The back of the postcard said: *Paiute Girl in Traditional Ceremonial Dress, 1970.*

The cowboy took his wig in his hand and shook it, brushing it the way he might brush a horse. "I'm supposed to send her money every month," he said. "But I don't. I'd be in prison stealing the money I'm supposed to send her. Last time I saw her she said those brothers of hers were out looking for me.

76

They're Tribal Police and they're allowed to kill me on sight, if they want."

The cowboy got quiet then and after a minute it looked like he was having trouble swallowing. Halfway through his eggs he turned and ran into the bathroom. When he came out he was sweaty and one of his eyes was deep red, like he'd poked it hard. I pointed to it and asked him what was wrong with it.

"Nothing's wrong with it," he said, looking peeved. "It's the other one."

The other was white, blue in the middle. "It looks fine," I said.

"It better. It cost six hundred dollars."

I looked at it again, and I was sorry that it looked so much better than the real one. He shook his head and poked around at his hard eggs, then he looked up at me.

"Goddamn, I'm scared to death of those Indians," he said. "It's so I can't even show up at a rodeo anymore, afraid they'll be there waiting. I don't even know what they look like. Every Indian I see has me reaching for my knife."

I didn't say anything. I was from Illinois and the thought of a cowboy this afraid of Indians impressed the hell out of me.

"I'm going to Texas," he said. "They got rodeo and I understand there's no Indians down there no more."

"Hell," I said. "I never seen a rodeo before. I'll go with you."

He didn't say anything. He picked up his cowboy hat and

put it on his head. I paid for the breakfast and got into the truck. We headed down south, meaning to catch the interstate by midday. We ate a few pills he had lying around in the truck, drank a few beers, partook of some weed. My head started buzzing and it got eerie when we dropped down and were in the desert officially. The valley we came into was hollow and flat, with carrier-shaped buttes on either side. Then suddenly down ahead of us lay the black ribbon of the interstate, with a few bright sparkles moving across the length of it. The highway we were on was rough and bumpy, and we bobbed around quite a bit in the little truck, but with the interstate in sight it looked like smooth sailing just ahead, all the way to Texas.

I was so grateful for the cowboy's company, and grateful for the truck and the interstate, and glad that I wouldn't be left in the desert alone to fend for myself. Things had been bad but they were looking up, looking up for the both of us. I would help him with his Indian problems and he would see me through the desert. Things were going to be fine, I was sure of it. Only, I hadn't noticed right off that the cowboy hadn't been saying much. I myself had been talking ever since breakfast about this and that, even about Cecil, of all things.

I should have paid more attention; it was five minutes later that the cowboy dumped me by the side of the road.

It was about thirty miles outside of Grand Junction that I saw the little white truck, pulled over to the side of the interstate, smoke billowing up from around the hood. It was nearly dark, and I turned off the lights of the Jeep. I could just see the cowboy off a ways into the desert, up against the wire fence, looking southeast toward Texas. He was a dark patch against the smooth white cover of the desert. I pulled up quiet behind the burning truck. I took the nine-millimeter from under the seat and, when I got out, stuffed it in the back waistband of my jeans. He hadn't even turned around.

I walked up to about ten feet behind him and cleared my throat. He turned slowly, and his face went confused when he saw me. He looked behind me at the Jeep. It was a few seconds before he looked me in the eye again. He was already scared and that suited me. I had liked him a lot but now I couldn't remember why.

"Hey, partner," he said. His voice was squeaky. "You come around just in time."

"Looks like it," I said.

He pointed with his good eye over at the smoldering truck. "Isn't that a bitch? Threw a rod."

"They'll do that."

"Yeah," he said, "they sure will. Where'd you get that Jeep?" He asked it in that way that didn't expect an answer. I just stared at him and didn't say anything. The light was nearly all gone and the gun was getting cold against my back. As he started to say something else I reached back and pulled it out. I figured it was the right time. He stopped right in his tracks.

"Hey," he said. "What's this for?"

"What's this for? You just took off, threw my bag onto the dirt and took off."

"You were talking crazy." His good eye darted around a little as he spoke, like it might have been following a fly. "Some wild faggot Navy shit about a drowned guy." As soon as he said this he licked his lips and his eyes slowed down. He reached behind and scratched the back of his neck. When he spoke again his voice was smoother. "You have to understand, I'm a wanted man. It wasn't anything personal."

I pointed the nine at his forehead. "Sounds personal as all get-out to me."

It had a good effect. His eyes went wide open and his mouth sort of dropped. He shook his head, and his eyes both stared at the pistol.

"You're with them Indians?" he said. His voice was high and terrified. "You are, aren't you?"

It was so crazy I wanted to laugh, but for some reason I couldn't. Instead I felt my throat start to tighten, and my eyes got blurry. The air had grown cold; I shivered. I waved the pistol side to side and made my voice hard.

"Kneel on the ground over here, back to me."

He came over slow and knelt in the dust in front of me, his back bowed, the knuckles of his spine pressed out under his T-shirt. He started to cry; his ribs pulsed out from his sides like gills, and he began to sway a little from side to side. I stepped up behind him, took off his hat, and put the nose of the gun gently against the back of his head, where his hair pulled together into the ponytail. Some white light flowed over him—a truck on the road behind us—and my shadow slid across his back. I pressed the gun against the soft underside of the ridge of his skull and his shoulders stiffened, his back arched, and he let out a small moan that made my head swirl.

"You should have never left like that," I said. "Why'd you do that?"

"God," he said, "tell her I'll come back, I promise."

"Hush, now." The hate was flowing from me, down into the dirt. "It's too late for her now." The sun had dropped and the air around us was now black, thick, and cold. My hands were numb and my legs ached.

"Here's what you do," I told him. "Just pretend you're swimming in the ocean." My voice was nearly a whisper. "You're swimming in the ocean, but you're getting weak." I heard him sob and I knew then that I wanted him to sink, that he *had* to sink. I lifted up the ponytail to do him at the top of the neck, quick and painless the way the Chinese do, and then I saw the empty slit in his collar. That did it; that did me in. I saw the slit and a chill began to rise in me, starting at my ankles and climbing me. My skin began to crawl; a quick shiver like an electric shock raced through me and then cracked like a whip along my spine. The pistol nearly tumbled from my fingers.

God the cowboy was fast. I didn't even see him whip around, I didn't see his hand when he stuck me in the thigh, high up by the pocket and hard into the bone where it wouldn't come out. I didn't see any of that, but I heard the nine snapping in my hand and then a howl and the sound of him running off into the desert. I dropped the gun into the dust and fell to the ground next to it. I curled up with my hands over my eyes, the handle of the knife prodding my belly.

After awhile I pulled my hands from my face and they stuck a little, coming away with a damp and sour smell. Through a paste in my eyes I could see the glowing outline of the truck through a pale light coming from the east. It was the moon rising over the desert, liquid and slow and steady. From far off I heard the boy calling for me, but a wind had come up, and he seemed to be crying; the sound rose and fell, rose and fell.

Hold on, I yelled out to him, *I'm coming*. Out on the road a semi-truck moaned past, eighty, ninety, and like an answer let off its horn, long and low. I felt around in the dust with my hand, my fingers found the gun; I closed my eyes and let the current take me out to him.

mr.
b*i*g
stuff

The Bandit moved into my back bedroom with little more than a shaving bag and a sorrowful expression on his potato face. His wife had gotten fed up and locked him out of his own home—shrewdly I thought—by simply stealing his house keys while he slept. She'd left him the ignition key to the Pinto, the small key to the locking gas cap (which had been lost months before), the extra key to the padlock on his son's bicycle (which had been stolen on the first day of school), and the key to the mailbox he had rented to sell flower seeds through small ads placed in the backs of women's magazines. The seeds scheme had started with an ad in the back of one of the men's magazines he read at the barbershop. "Make money from your home," it had stated. "Small investment. Millions of women read." He had sent twenty dollars for the details, mostly for an explanation of how women reading could translate into extra income. But just when he'd gotten started he discovered that his seventeen-year-old son had been eating the seeds on the sly; in a panic the Bandit flushed his entire inventory down the toilet. When he got to that point in the story I stopped him and began pulling the cushions from the couch.

"Lay these on the floor in there," I said. "There's a sleeping bag in the closet." It was the best I could do. I had sold all the furniture in the spare bedroom, the couch did not convert into anything, and my spare top-sheets were draped over the curtain rod above my balcony door.

"Where did you park?" I said.

"I don't know." He yawned and blinked at the cushions stacked in my arms. "Out back somewhere."

"Where?"

"I don't know. Next to that wooden pen where the Dumpsters are."

"In a numbered space?"

"I think so."

"Shit," I said, handing him the cushions. I walked to the balcony door and pulled aside the sheet. Down in the parking lot the Bandit's Pinto sat under a yellow streetlight. Security had already stickered it. As usual, they'd placed the sticker on the driver's side of the windshield, and I knew from experience that the glue they used made the stickers extremely hard to scrape off. If they traced the Pinto to me I'd get a form letter from the Board and a bill for twenty-five dollars, payable with the next month's rent.

"In the morning go out the back door and around the side," I told him. "They may be watching so don't look up at the window. And park on the street from now on."

He was already heading down the hall to the back bedroom, the seat of his trousers hanging off his rear in a baggy crease that see-sawed as he walked. He clutched the cushions awkwardly against his chest, and as he passed through the bedroom doorway he brushed against the side, causing a brief, weary ricochet between the jambs. He dropped the cushions on the bedroom floor and closed the door behind him.

Fred the Bandit was the only acquaintance I had left from the previous winter, my insurance-selling days, before I had taken so many personal days they stopped sending me a check and instead sent the state-mandated form for continuing my health coverage through my own monthly contributions. Fred the Bandit had loaned me money back then when I needed it, before unemployment had kicked in. Even though we had fallen out of touch somewhat since then, when the Bandit called me from the convenience store of course I said yes; to say anything else would have been heartless. He must have been desperate to call me. He thanked me; he told me I was a good man. I could hear the video games sizzling and popping in the background. But no spitting tobacco, I told him. Chewing plugs of Bandit tobacco was how he'd gotten his nickname—an ill fit for a pudgy, balding Life and Health rep. I'd seen his filthy brown spit cups sitting around the garage. No wonder his wife had locked him out.

The first scream came at one-seventeen in the morning. The second scream was louder than the first, riper with dull terror, and hung on longer, with a sharp sucking sob at the end.

"Bandit," I yelled. "Jesus Christ."

He answered with another scream, this one lower, more despairing. I climbed out of bed in my jockeys, trotted down the hall, and rapped softly on the door to the rear bedroom just as he started a fourth. I knew better than to startle someone out of a nightmare; gentleness was called for. The knock was effective; the fourth scream trailed off in the middle with a short, snuffling *huh*. I pressed open the door. The Bandit lay on his back on the cushions; his face and neck stuck out of the sleeping bag like a pale toe from a dark sock. His eyes were wide and black, and his broad forehead glistened in the amber light from the parking lot.

"What's going on?" he said thickly. "Who is it?"

"It's you," I said. "You were having a nightmare." I started to close the door.

"Wow," he said. He scratched an armpit. "No kidding? What was I saying?"

"You weren't saying anything. You were just screaming bloody murder."

"It's night terror," he said, with a touch of awe in his voice. "Man. I haven't had it since college."

"Terrific," I said. I closed the door. I seldom had nightmares, but when I did I could never get back to sleep, afraid not really of bad dreams but of being afraid—the fear of fear itself, so to speak. I would lie on my bed waiting for the morning like a child, pointing my eyes at the ceiling to keep them open. Only when the morning finally came would I try to sleep. But naturally I couldn't; I was too ashamed of myself.

There was nothing to be done. I put on my coat, killed the lights, and slipped out the front door.

About a mile from my apartment complex, just across the invisible boundary that marks the frontier of Palatine, Illinois, was a brown-brick country-western dive we just called the Chili Place because we could never remember the real name and they had the only neon sign advertising chili I had ever seen. CHILI HERE it said in mismatched blood-red lettering, inside a bowl-shaped border. The chili sign was a beacon so bright and red it outshone the beer signs on either side of it.

I found a stool open at one end of the horseshoe-shaped bar; as soon as I sat down the guy next to me pointed at me with his thumb and said, "Him, too."

"Me too what?" I said. The bartender slapped a soggy coaster on the bar in front of me and covered it with a bottle of beer.

"That's what," the bartender said. "Don't be a gift horse."

I watched the bartender set bottles in front of a dozen or so other drinkers; for one slacker he up-ended a shot glass. "You got one on ice, Delbert," he said. Delbert, a fat man with a pool stick in his fist, nodded at the guy next to me. One or two of the others tipped the throats of their bottles at him.

"I guess that was you that won the lottery, then," I said to my benefactor. "How does it feel?"

"Tell you one thing," he said, "if I did win the lottery? Me? I wouldn't be one of those dumbshits who don't quit their

89

fucking jobs, that's for sure." He had a thick black beard and little translucent yellow-gray teeth lined up like rows of un-popped popcorn. He was the kind of white man you'd find in a cheap movie about Arab terrorists.

"You've got to have a job to quit it," I said. "I'm not cur-rently blessed with such a problem."

"I got something easy for you to do, then," he said. "Drink any beer that God puts in front of you. Knock them off the face of the earth."

"The problem with that is I got exactly five dollars," I said.

"How do you expect to pick up a woman with only five dollars?" interjected Delbert from behind his pool cue.

"Technique," I said.

The bearded guy slid some cash along the bar toward me. "Hey," he said, not smiling. "You always talk so much on the job?" I pretended not to notice the money, but after a moment I adjusted my chair so I was sitting more directly behind it.

One of the other drinkers leaned closer; a fortyish guy in a cap with USS Something sewn in gold above the brim. "He likes to talk so much, have him talk to them," he said. He nod-ded across the oval bar at two young women, one blond and pretty and the other brunette and not, drinking wine coolers out of the bottle and smoking.

"Maybe later," I said. "I should tell you all, though, the women who come here usually aren't looking for company."

"They look friendly enough to me," Delbert said. He tipped his bottle in their direction; neither responded. "See what I mean? Women are the same everywhere."

90

"Where do you usually hang out?" I asked the bearded guy.

"Over by O'Hare," he said. "Place called the Idle Hour. But we've had it with that place. Bad luck."

"What kind of bad luck?"

"Well," he said, "there was Jerry B. almost choking to death on that chicken wing."

"Almost," I said. "I guess that means he lived."

"Yeah, just the busted rib was all," said Delbert. "Some guy Heimliched him." He winced with the recollection. "Biker, I think he was." I began to like him. He was chubby and agreeable—excellent sidekick material. Not for me, but for someone.

"That's not all," said the bearded guy. "There was one dumbshit got involved with the wrong woman there. Cost him."

Delbert's face lost some of its brightness.

"He was just sitting there minding his own business and she was sitting across the bar, say about where Bignose is sitting over there," he said. "She comes over and asks him if he could give her change for the jukebox, so he says why me."

"What did she say?"

"She said she thought he picked good songs. The thing is, he never played the jukebox once and she knew it. She had him scoped out from the word go. It was all strictly BS, pure bullshit."

"Love is strange," I said. "I knew a guy once—"

"You going to let me finish?"

"I'm sorry," I said.

"Did that sound like the end of the story?" He swiveled sharply in his seat. "Give him another beer," he said to the bartender. "Keep his mouth busy."

"So what happened? Did he leave with her?"

He turned back around and pretended to get tired of his own story. "Leave, shit," he said. "No reason to leave."

"Idle Hour stays open till four," Delbert said. He leaned his stick up against the bar and began talking with his hands.

"You see, the way it works is you get Ronnie to sell you a six right before five o'clock and then you sit in the parking lot. Ronnie's wife comes in at six and opens her back up. Best thing is to get a little companionship—that way you've got yourself a sweet little one-hour interlude there in the backseat. Follow that up with a piss and a boatswain's breakfast and you're ready to start all over again."

"What's a boatswain's breakfast?"

"Cigarette and a puke," said Delbert, looking proud of himself.

The bearded guy cut us off. "I'm not finished with my story," he said.

"I don't think I want to hear the rest," I said. "You're going to tell me she did all thirteen of you guys at the same time or something greasy like that."

"Nope," he said. "It was just her and the one dumbshit. The two of them hopped in a Buick and they just stayed in there when Ronnie's wife opened the doors back up. We came out at nine and found him lying in the backseat by him-self, dead as a hammer."

"Wow, pretty stupid," I said. A few of the drinkers stopped talking and looked at me.

"Now why would you say that?" the bearded guy asked.

"I don't know," I said. "I mean, it's common knowledge that running your heater in one spot is dangerous. Carbon monoxide poisoning."

"What heater? What exhaust? Car wasn't running."

"What do you—he had a heart attack or something?"

"Not to my knowledge."

Delbert took this opportunity to intervene. "Don't listen to this guy," he said to me. "Nobody died. Fact is, the two of them got married. Moved to Florida."

"Same thing, brother," the bearded guy said.

Something had been tightening in my chest, and now it slacked off. "Don't tell me happy ever after?" I said.

"Shiiit, no," the bearded guy said. "Ol' Del ditched the cunt in Clearwater and moved back up here to be with the boys again. Didn't you, Delbert?"

Delbert shrugged. "I ditched her, she ditched me. Who keeps track?"

I shook my head. "You gentlemen have it all worked out, that's for sure."

"What's that supposed to mean?"

"Nothing," I said.

"Hey, Charlie, get my friend here another drink."

"Pass," I said. "Really." The bartender went back to cleaning glasses.

"What, Mr. Big Stuff, won't take a drink?" the bearded guy said.

"He doesn't like us anymore," Delbert said.

"I'm sorry. Maybe I should just sit over here." I scooted my stool back to where I had found it, away from the money the bearded guy had left on the bar. But he saw my eyes flit down and back.

"You want it?" he said. "Here." He walked up to me and started stuffing the cash from the bar into the neck of my sweatshirt. I felt his cold and wet knuckles on my throat. I twisted away, clutching the neck of my sweatshirt as if protecting myself from a masher. "Stop it," I cried. My voice came out high and strained.

"Stop it," he mimicked—a falsetto.

Delbert stepped forward. "Peace, brothers," he said, his face solemn. "Let's all get along with the locals."

I picked up my beer and retreated to the jukebox on the other side of the bar. I passed the two women and made it a point not to look at them. I read every song title, playing none, without turning around. When I was done I fed a pinball machine and nursed my beer.

don't know how much time I killed, but after an hour or so I was distracted by some commotion from the other end of the bar— a knot of people stood, a woman's voice wailed. Delbert stood on the outside of the knot, his pool cue in front of him like a staff. I went over; they were all looking at the floor, upon which lay the blond woman, dark blood leaking from her forehead. Everybody stood as if in an enormous huddle, silently looking down, except for one guy who crouched over her with his hands on his knees and her companion, the big-nosed brunette, who began to scream in rapid-fire bursts, like a cheer.

The people in front of me parted easily to let me through. The croucher glanced back at me and relinquished his place with a grateful look. Someone killed the jukebox—in the hollow silence the big-nosed brunette's voice sharpened but it didn't make much difference; whatever she was saying might easily have been in another language. I was suddenly the closest one to her, to the injured blonde, and there was nothing else to do but kneel down and take her hand. It was warm and light.

"Hey," I said. "Hey, it's all right. You just had a little fall." Her sides were pulsing in and out, and she was breathing hard through her nose.

"Hey, can you hear me?" I said. Her eyes opened and locked briefly on mine before detaching and raking across the room.

"Don't go into shock, now," I said, stupidly. I rubbed her forearm clumsily with my free hand.

Bignose stopped screaming and took a breath. "Little fall? He hit her," she shouted in the general direction of everyone in the bar. "He just walked up and hit her with a bottle." She leaned down, teetering a little. She reached out her hand as if to touch her friend's forehead and then pulled it back. "God," she said. "I don't believe it."

"Take it easy," I said. I raised my arm to ward her off in case she fell on top of us. "Why don't you go sit down?"

She ignored me. "We're going to the hospital, Ginnie," she said. "We're going to the hospital and when we get there we'll have a party, honey. Don't you worry."

Ginnie's eyes and nose started to run; clear streams that flowed out and down the sides of her face. Higher up on her head the blood had welled up and then it, too, ran down her temple and onto the floor, like a fat red pendant. Her breath rattled in the back of her throat.

"Get me a towel or something," I called to the bartender. "A handkerchief." He blinked and then threw a bar rag over to me with an underhand flip. I caught it in midair; it was gray and damp. "A fucking clean towel," I said. Someone handed me a bandanna. It looked passably clean so I folded it and touched it to Ginnie's forehead. Blood seemed to leap onto it, soaking right in. I dabbed carefully crossways; when I lifted the bandanna, it seemed awfully heavy, but Ginnie's forehead underneath was pale and unmarked.

"Hold still," I whispered to her. I let go of Ginnie's hand, and with either forefinger I gently parted her hair. I could feel her take in a breath and hold it, but she didn't stop me, didn't object or pull her head away. Just about an inch above her widow's peak was a small gash, edges slightly separated, and no longer than a fingernail. Dark blood clung to the sides, solid as gelatin. It oozed a tiny bit, but nothing more seemed to be flowing out.

"Ginnie," I said. "You've got a small cut up on your forehead, but it's above your hairline. You won't even have a scar that anyone will see. It's really not so bad."

She stared at me, and then raised her hands and looked at them. "But there's so much blood. Is this all mine?"

"Head wounds bleed a lot," I said. "Trust me, it's going to be okay. Just don't get excited. It's stopped bleeding already."

"But there's so much," she said.

"Are you cold?" I asked her. She didn't answer. After a moment she dropped her arms back to her side. I took her hand again and she pressed my fingers.

"I'm not cold," she said. "I'm all right."

This statement seemed to break a spell; people began to mill around again. The girlfriend settled back on her stool and began rustling suspiciously through the contents of Ginnie's purse. Ginnie took a few breaths and started to rise.

"Whoa," I said. My free hand pressed down on her shoulder.

"Why can't I get up?" she said. "I just want to sit."

"It'll start bleeding again. Head wounds bleed a lot."

"You said that already," said Ginnie.

The girlfriend leaned in over my shoulder. "Just lie there, sweetie, they'll be here in a minute." It was the first intelligent thing she had contributed. She choked back a sob. "They're on their way, baby."

Ginnie started to cry, again, softly. "Can't I get up off the floor?" she said, pressing my hand. "It's dirty down here. It smells." Her fingers loosened in mine but I kept a firm hold.

"Now, Virginia . . ." I said, trying to sound soothing.

"Who?" she said.

"That's not her name," the girlfriend said. "It's Jennifer." She had finished wiping her nose and was acting suspicious again.

"Jenny," the woman said from below. She had also stopped crying. "And I'm getting up off this floor."

Just then a stocky guy hunkered down next to me and shouldered me aside. I almost toppled over. I squared myself to shove him back when an arm went around my shoulders from the opposite direction. It was a cop in a black leather jacket, squatting next to me.

"Let's let the man work, what do you say, pal?" he said. The guy on the other side shouldered me again and this time I saw he had paramedic patches on his sleeves. He was crouched over looking at Ginnie's eyeballs, his thumb pulling up her eyelid, a penlight flipping back and forth across her pupil.

"Okay?" the cop said. His arm tightened on my shoulder.

"Okay," I said.

"So let go of her hand, buddy."

I looked down and sure enough my hand was still wrapped in hers. The paramedic had stopped what he was doing and he and Ginnie stared at me. I let go and the paramedic took her hand and laid it professionally on her stomach, palm up. He eyed his watch and his fingertips feathered her fine, blue-white wrist. She stared up at him and when he caught her eye he smiled.

"So what's your name, honey?" he asked.

"Fuck you," Ginnie said.

The cop walked me outside. I thought there might be a lineup for me to examine, a statement to give. The parking lot was nearly empty. Under a streetlight the girlfriend was standing and shivering next to a white police car with black doors. For the first time I noticed she was very tall, almost taller than the cop. I considered offering to drive her to the hospital, or to follow her in the ambulance and drive her back, some such chivalry.

When she saw me walking up she pointed at me. "Him," she said. "He knows him."

"What's the name," the cop said.

"Bergman," I said. "With an 'e.' "

"Where does he live?"

"Where does who live?"

The girlfriend cut in. "Your buddy. The one with the broken bottle, the son-of-a-bitch." A soggy hiccup caught in her throat but she fought it off. She seemed to be sobering up fast.

I looked at the cop but he just stared at me, waiting for an answer.

"I never saw him before," I said. "He was just some drunk. I can give you a description, but no name. I never asked."

"All right," the cop said. "Give me a description."

"He had a beard. A black beard and a funny eye. I think it was glass."

"Not him," Bignose said. "The other one, the chubby guy. He had a . . . what do you call it? A pool cue."

It was all I could do to not say his name out loud. I looked thoughtful for a second and then shrugged. "Guess I'm out of the loop on this one," I said. The cop closed his notebook.

The girlfriend started crying again in a snorting, frustrated way. "Bullshit," she said to the cop. "He was talking to him all night long."

But the cop was already walking back to the doorway. "Look," he said over his shoulder. "All I know is when I showed up this guy was the only one doing anything. Maybe he's the good guy. You ever think of that?"

The girlfriend shook her head as if just remembering something important. "No, wait, they gave you money," she said, staring at me. "People just don't give money to strangers." But the cop was already inside. She stared at me for a few more seconds, then took a step toward me.

"When you see your friend, tell him he's a big man," she said. I was afraid she was going to hit me or scratch at my face. I stepped back. "Tell him he's a big individual," she said. "Big man, put a girl in the hospital. Tell him that for me."

"I'm not going to see him," I said. "I told you, I don't know him. Jesus, I don't believe this."

"Oh, save it," she said. She suddenly wasn't crying, she wasn't sobbing. She just stood there, examining me. I was glad she wasn't beautiful; it was bad enough she was so tall.

She stepped close again, and again I retreated. I was almost up against the police car.

100

"Different this way, isn't it?" she said. "Standing out here like this?"

I closed my eyes. "I don't know him," I whispered. When I opened my eyes she had already walked away, following the cop. I got in my car and tried not to hurry too much out of the parking lot. I turned on my lights halfway down the block.

When I got back to the apartment complex someone had taken my parking spot. I took a Visitor's spot, even though that, too, was against the rules. Inside the apartment it was so dark I turned on all the lights just to get the lateness out of the air. It took me a second to make out a strange noise; low moans leaking down the hall from the rear bedroom.

"Oh, Jesus Jumping Christ," I said.

At the end of the hall I pushed open the bedroom door and turned on the light. The Bandit was writhing inside his sleeping bag with his eyes squeezed tight, his face gray in the yellow glare of the streetlight. He seemed to be trying to get his hands up to protect himself but he'd gotten them trapped in the sleeping bag. While I watched he twisted hard and tumbled off the cushion onto his side. He squirmed across the floor like some kind of gigantic, moaning pupa. I was tempted to kick him, just kick him to his feet. Instead I slammed the door hard behind me and went into the bathroom to wash the blood from my hands.

The bathroom mirror was full—occupied by a stranger with bleary eyes, bad skin, and a stooped, bar-hunch posture. I leaned closer. There was blood in a streak across my face and several swipes across the front of my shirt that had dried to a rusty brown. I raised the shirt to my nose and sniffed; possibly I had expected perfume, but Ginnie's blood smelled rank. I yanked the dirty shirt off over my head and a half-dozen dollar bills fluttered down around my shoulders like ashes at a house fire. I stared at them, not quite comprehending, and was still staring when there came a soft rap on the bathroom door. Without thinking I snatched the bills up off the linoleum, threw them in the toilet, and pulled the handle. I waited, holding my breath, as the tank filled back up, afraid the money would clog the drain. The Bandit's voice came hushed through the door, asking me if everything was okay.

"Yeah," I said, looking around me. I sat down on the edge of the tub. "I'm just going to take a bath." I waited for the Bandit to move away from the door. "Thanks, buddy," I said.

There was a silent moment when I was sure he would never leave the goddamn hallway. "Sorry if I scared you," he said, finally. I heard his feet slap lightly on the floor and then the sound of the bedroom door closing.

I looked at my watch. Five-fifty. One hour at least until dawn. I ran water into the tub, mainly for effect, and sat on the toilet lid. A bath would be nice, but I couldn't risk it. Warm water might make me sleepy, and I couldn't take the chance. Even lying down would be asking for it. I raised my eyes, found a spot on the ceiling—a water stain from the floor above—and waited.

outstanding
in my
field

didn't like college at first so I dropped out to go back and be with my friends full time. I got my old job back at the Target store, putting together bikes that came off the truck already partly assembled and stuffed inside wide, flat boxes. I was good at it; good and fast. Although Hardware was just two aisles over I used only the simplest tools: pliers, crescent wrench, stubby Phillips screwdriver. Often I ended up with spare parts left over—washers and nuts and the odd piece of chrome—and I kept them in a box in case someone came back to complain. Nobody ever did. The people who bought bicycles at Target back then weren't the type to come back and complain. They most likely took it out on the kids.

I lived in a trailer in the middle of a field. Both the field and the trailer were green. My landlord lived a half a mile or so across the field, up against the highway. His name was Greer, and one of my friends—drunk, no doubt, because he thought it was hilarious—dubbed the place Greer's Acres. (I dreamt about the trailer just last night. In the dream the trailer was impossibly small, the size of a refrigerator on its side. Once you crawled in it seemed larger. In the dream Greer—no older—explained that it had been renovated, which was why it was unrecognizable.) Back then Greer always spoke musingly of renovations he had in the works; how he was going to replace the broken windows, build a wooden deck off the front, put ornamental siding around the base to hide the wheels and weeds underneath. All he succeeded in doing was, for reasons he never explained, rotating the entire thing ninety degrees so that the trailer and its brown dirt shadow made an X in the field. I had no water for a week, and when I did the sinks and toilet drained right onto the ground beneath me with a disgusting noise. Greer worked slowly, but hooking up the septic line was one thing he accomplished in a hurry.

It was the summer of Mt. St. Helens. Thirty days in a row over one hundred degrees, and the thermometer stayed above eighty through the night. Old people dropped dead in their living rooms. Cars without air-conditioning went undriven. The city pool was body temperature. Every night after work my friends swerved their cars off the highway and charged across my rutted field to the trailer, wheels hammering up and down beneath their fenders, 8-track stereos blaring. They came in their Impalas, Malibus, Novas—there were no Fords. They brought beer, hamburgers, speed, blotter acid, a pistol. They brought me charcoal, folding chairs, a small black-and-white television, *Penthouses*, antifreeze for my leaky Dodge, No-Pest strips, fuses, and bags of ice. We put the least poisonous of it in our mouths and jumped and shook and yelled and broke windows and lit small fires and tore up linoleum and cussed and hugged and wrestled and threw up and watched the small black-and-white television till all hours. In the morning they were gone and I slept until the heat drove me into the dark shade of the bathroom to retch and shower.

Of course I was in love with my best friend's girlfriend, Lorraine. It was an open secret between the three of us, never discussed. It was as if we had borne a child in secret who—since it looked exactly like me—was left to me to care for. I nursed that baby, knowing full well that when the two of them were together they did not think much about the baby and me sitting alone in the trailer. I was more aware of the nobility of my situation than perhaps they were.

Sometimes Lorraine visited me in my trailer during the heat of the day. She sat at my little Formica table and asked me what it was I thought I was doing. She asked me about the engineering scholarship I had abandoned. I told her how I had lost my job putting together bicycles at the Target store when a wheel fell off at the checkout lane. I told her how I had plans to get my brother's Firebird away from his ex-girlfriend so I could sell it and live on the money. Lorraine fanned herself silently and perspired in the hollow of her throat. I cannot remember what she wore. When I think about it now I see her in something a twenty-year-old seductress would wear today, which would be historically inaccurate. Perhaps she wore cut-off shorts, or those high-waisted polyester hot pants. I sat in a vinyl chair and talked with confidence about myself. She listened and looked at me as if waiting for something. She never let on to what that might be and she never stayed more than ten minutes. She was, after all, just checking up on the baby.

It was a mid-month sweltering weekday when the wrestler showed up, knocking up at my front door, which had swung out flat against the aluminum side of the trailer. It was stuck that way—someone had been swinging on it and now it didn't close at all. The guy was probably thirty years old, with red hair and a face best described as apple-cheeked and Huck Finnish. He wore a blue muscle shirt and some kind of denim shorts. He was barefoot, standing on the grass beneath my single wooden step. Something about him looked vaguely familiar. When I stuck my head out of the doorway I didn't see a car. "How's it going?" I asked him. I didn't say anything about his coming in.

"You know where I can find that guy I was out here with the other night?" he said.

"You were out here the other night?" I looked around again for a car and again I didn't see one. Nobody ever walked to my trailer; it was just too far from everything to walk to. "Which night?"

"The other night. There were dogs running around, and some people were dancing up on the propane tank."

"Are you that guy from California?"

"No," he said. "The guy who jumped up and down on his car top is who you're thinking of."

"Oh," I said. "You want a glass of water?"

"No thanks," he said, "I was just wondering about that guy."

"Never saw him before. From California you said?"

"Not him. I'm talking about the guy who drove the white truck. The rusty white truck with the winch." He was smiling but smiling that way that people do when they're preparing to be disappointed.

"That would be Russ," I said. "He's probably working." Russ was someone I didn't know too well, the brother of one of the girls who sometimes hung around with us. He was a farmer's kid, bright and healthy and strong. We didn't let him drink because when he got drunk he hit his head against walls and cars and tree trunks and cried into the crook of his elbow. "I'm going to Hell," he would cry, "I'm just going straight to Hell." He was religious and hard on himself.

"Do you know where he works?"

"On his old man's farm, out by the Air Force base. I forget which road."

The guy sighed and sat down on my single wooden step. His hair was so thin and red I could see his pink scalp through it. I believe his whole head may have been freckled.

"I don't suppose you wrestle, do you," he said, still sitting and looking away across my field.

"Now I remember you," I said. "You're that wrestler, that country-style wrestler guy." He had shown up a few nights earlier with some people I barely knew, stayed for some indeterminate length of time, spoke with me about something, and left when everyone else left. Many hundreds of people just like him came to my field that summer, or perhaps a dozen.

"Appalachian style," he said, getting to his feet. Just saying the words seemed to brighten him up. "We're trying to get it into the schools."

"Get what into the schools?"

"Our wrestling style. It's better, safer. It's more traditional, a hundred percent American."

"How so?" The questions were sort of sliding out of my mouth without much effort behind them. It was something to do.

"Well," he said, "there's no holds below the waist, for one."

"Like sumo," I said. "Or what is it, that other thing . . . Greco-Roman."

He looked a little annoyed. "Kind of like that. Not so much bullshit, though."

"That's good," I said.

"You ever wrestle?" He looked me over like a tailor. "What are you, six-two, one-sixty-five?"

"No," I said. "Yeah but no."

"It's a good weight. You'd have leverage with your height. Most guys would be way under six foot."

"You need to be strong," I said. "I don't have time for that."

"You need to have leverage," he said. "You don't need to be all that strong." As he said this I couldn't help but notice the muscles in his shoulders bunched a little along the top, like mattress ticking. I knew a little about leverage myself, and this seemed like baloney. "You do need to be smart, though," he rattled on. "Keep your power position. Know your opponent."

"I don't have time to practice that kind of thing."

He looked behind me at the empty trailer and nodded. A little smile slid across his mouth. "I'll take that glass of water now," he said.

"Inside or outside?"

"How about inside. I'm frying out here." He came up the wooden step and into the heavy shade of the trailer. He sat at my Formica table and I filled a glass for him. The glass had the logo of a football team on one side and one of Pizza Hut on the other. I had five of them, but only two different teams. I had gotten sick of their pizza while still in the NFC Central.

"Well water," I said. "It's pretty cold."

He took a drink. "Oh, yes," he said. "That could give you a headache." He sat and sipped at it like tea. When he swallowed, his apple cheeks popped out a little at me.

"I pour it over me and sit in front of the fan," I said. "Works pretty good."

"Put it against your carotid artery." He held his glass against the side of his neck. "Cools the blood to your brain and you fool your whole body."

"I thought that was your jugular," I said.

"Most people think that," he said. "That's a common misconception."

I filled up a glass and held it against my carotid artery.

Nothing much happened. Tepid water condensed off the glass and ran unpleasantly down over my collarbone.

"A lot of stuff like that doesn't work for me," I said.

He smiled again in a knowing way. He sat in his chair with his knees apart and looked around the trailer appraisingly. "Looks better at night," he said. "It's like a little island out here with the lights and everything. Or more like a ship out on the ocean. All the little windows and all."

"Sounds like the ocean with the highway out there," I said. "I'm into the solitude."

"Really?" he said. "I thought you were Mr. Party."

He was beginning to annoy me. "Where's your car?" I asked him. "How'd you get way out here?"

"I walked," he said. He stood up and pointed out the open doorway. "See that little green house over there?" He pointed to a clump of trees about a half mile up the highway, the opposite direction from my landlord's house. "That's my house."

"Oh, yeah?" I said. "I wondered who lived there." I had wondered because often I saw a man standing in the yard staring across the field at my trailer. This was before Greer had turned the thing. I would look out the front window and see him standing there for the longest time. He stood in his weedy yard in front of his tiny green house and stared. Apparently he had decided to quit staring and just come on over.

"It's Greer's," he said. "He owns all of this. Whole thing used to be a bean farm."

"Maybe that's why he paints everything green," I said.

Right then he turned quickly to me. "Let's try out a few holds, what do you say?"

I opened my mouth and laughed politely down in my throat, not right in his face the way I should have. "I don't think so," I said.

"Come on," he said. "You got nothing better to do."

"Forget it."

"Why not? Give me a reason."

"It's unfair," I said, even though the real reason was I didn't feel like it. "You've got twenty pounds of muscle on me, for one thing. Plus you know the shit and I don't."

He leaned across the table. "Here," he said. He put his elbow on the tabletop and held his hand up in front of me. "Let me get an idea of your strength. Come on."

I sighed and put my hand in his. I could tell the way he gripped it that he was one of those serious arm wrestlers who tried to win with the wrist. I gave up before I started.

"Go," he said. I pushed against his hand with about two thirds of my strength. It moved several inches. He looked at me, surprised.

"That it?"

"Hey," I said, letting go of his hand. "I told you I didn't go for this."

"Don't tell me," he said. "You're a lover, not a fighter."

In hindsight that's one of the things that irritated me about him, but I didn't know it just then. He shouldn't have been in my trailer, teasing me like that. It was a breach of etiquette that was apparently over his head.

"Remember," he said, standing up then dropping to his knees on the linoleum. "Nothing with the legs. Arms only."

"You see?" I said, still sitting in my chair. "That's just it. The way you wrestler guys start out looks a little funny, if you know what I mean."

"Forget about that," he said. "Remember, without holding the legs it's more leverage and weight distribution than strength. Come on." He went down on his hands and gave me a head-jerk behind him as if all I needed was to know which direction I was supposed to go.

"It's too hot," I said. But I made the mistake of putting my glass down with too much finality, the way someone does when they're getting up. We both saw it.

"Come on," he said. "Learn something."

I went over and kneeled in the spot where he had nodded, which was behind him and slightly to one side. I sat back on my heels and sighted up the shelf of his back. His shoulder blades hunched up and there was a deep channel down the middle of his spine. Inside the channel his blue shirt was pocked with deeper blue oblong shapes where perspiration had seeped through. Underneath him the shirt fell loosely away from his chest and stomach. The soles of his feet were stained a golden color from the weeds in my field.

He instructed me where to put my knees, where to put my chin, how to grab the top of his wrist. I moved up onto his back and things went fast then. I honestly cannot remember all of the details now—he took it easy on me, I'm sure. When he flipped me he made sure I did not hit the walls.

When he pinned me he did not stay on top of me for long. I did not know what I was doing and he handled me as if I were a small child, as close to tenderly as was probably possible given the circumstances. He was true to his word and used leverage to defeat me, not his advantage in strength. I struggled against every part of him, and every part of him was firmly lodged; I might as well have been trying to pin myself. We wrestled for fifteen minutes and we both knew somehow when it was time to quit. We got to our feet, soaked with sweat and with red and splotchy skin, and went back to the little Formica table.

"I have a confession to make," he said. We had only been sitting for a few seconds. He was breathing deeply and rolling his shoulders.

"So confess," I said uneasily.

"I used to live in this trailer," he said. "Couple of years ago."

It wasn't one of the things I thought he might be confessing, to tell you the truth, but it made me feel sick to my stomach. That and the heat. I didn't answer him and we sat and panted for a while and didn't say anything more. I almost rather he'd told me he was some pervert with a good cover story who wandered around the country pinning perfect strangers to their own floors. I couldn't think of anything to say to this.

Once he got his breath back he started talking again. "So," he said, "you think you'll go back to school or what?" He looked around at the broken windows. He was my close

115

buddy now. "You should. There's nothing here, believe me. You may not know it now, but this place gets mighty goddamn cold in the winter."

"I don't know," I said. "I've got this girlfriend."

"Yeah, yeah, I know about her," he said with a little wave of his hand.

I looked at him.

"You forget we've spoken before." He shook his head dismissively. "Memory loss at such a young age. You should really go back to college."

"What's it to you what I do?"

He shrugged and picked up his glass and finished the water. He looked out the window again.

"Can't get used to the view this way," he said. "I look out and expect to see the highway and forget the whole thing's been turned." He looked back at me. "I see her drive up," he said. "And I see her go." His eyes were kinder now. "You can't miss a thing like that way out here."

We were quiet for a moment. I looked down and one of my hands was gripping the skinny leg of the little Formica table. I wondered if he knew I wanted to break the table over his head. Sure he did. He knew because he stood up to leave me just like that. He opened his mouth to say something but I'd anticipated him and got in first.

"You know, he won't be back around here ever," I said. "I barely know him, matter of fact."

He looked surprised. More than surprised. "Well, he might," he said.

"I really, really doubt it."

He gave a little laugh. He looked down at the empty glass on the table in front of him. "Anyway," he said softly, "if he does . . ."

"Whatever," I said.

"Well," he said. "See you, I guess."

"Take care," I said. I shouldn't have been smiling but I was. My hand relaxed on the table leg.

He stepped down out of the trailer and walked off across the field. I watched him go, all the way to his little green shack of a house and inside. It took him a while, and I wondered if I'd actually managed to hurt him a little back there. He had a funny walk, like he was very careful where he placed his feet. Not that I could really blame him—he was barefoot and there was no telling what we had left lying around out there to step on. It was like a minefield out there. He really should have worn shoes—that was another thing about him.

the blue norton

never had a sex-only relationship. Other people had them, the guy who lived above me on Johnson Street had one, with a woman who would sometimes show up when he wasn't even home. Other times when she walked up the outside steps and rapped on his screen door he just plain didn't answer—I knew he was home because I heard him start walking around again after she gave up and left. Maybe he had someone else up there at the time. I couldn't be sure; it's hard to distinguish the footsteps of a single person from those of a couple, unless they're on opposite sides of the room. A party, yes; a couple, no.

I had *things* with women: I had a thing with a lawyer I met at a Gulf War protest. She used to make me go out, just before we went to bed, and get a bottle of wine, even if we already had one handy. I had a thing with a bartender who lived in a motel and called her kids long-distance. They were in Alaska purse-seining with their father, who was supposed to send them home with lots of cash. I had a thing with a professor's wife. She was a professor too, so I guess I had a thing with a professor, but it didn't feel that way. If she had been *my* professor, I couldn't have done it. The whole time I'd be

121

thinking, "Jesus Christ, this is a *professor*," and it wouldn't have worked. Once I label a person something, it sticks in my mind.

But these things were not sex-only relationships. In each case we did many things besides have sex. With the lawyer I went to concerts and recitals and poetry readings. The bartender liked to drive and liked to shop, so we did a lot of day trips to outlet centers and places like the Amana Colonies, where you can eat knockwurst and see where they invented the microwave. The professor's wife and I golfed and canoed along the river by the arts buildings, which was how the professor found out about us, as was her intention all along.

So when I finally did get into a sex-only relationship, I felt both awkward and relieved; awkward because the woman was so single-minded about the sex, relieved because her single-mindedness kept me from having to endure the outlet malls, the golf, and the deceit.

She was not pretty. You might say she was ruggedly handsome, attractive in an oddly virile way, like a tough cowgirl in a bad western. Except this one wasn't going to turn up a few weeks later as a Southern belle or a Philadelphia debutante. She was exactly who she was. If you want to know the truth, she looked and acted like a dyke. She had a kind of flattop haircut, a stud in one nostril, and wore a lot of camouflage colors in her wardrobe. And she was solid. No jiggle, no soft fleshy folds to nuzzle—her body was as tight as a dolphin's. It was also about as curvy. Even in a halter top she looked like she belonged in Special Forces.

Except for her hands. They were tiny, delicate things; perfect nails with lovely white crescent moons, soft knuckles that looked like the closed eyes of sleeping babes. Her hands became the most important part of her. I developed a mild hand fetish, I think; they were that spectacular. I couldn't tell you what my previous lovers' hands were like—they might have been flippers for all I remember.

I wasn't quiet about it, either. "You have awesome hands," I told her once. "Just . . . I don't know, great fucking hands."

"So I've heard," she said, with a chill in her voice. It was as though I'd told her she had great tits. It made me think twice about complimenting her on anything else, like her eyes or even her terrific voice, which was both husky and soft. It wasn't altogether feminine, though. More like a twelve-year-old boy with his first hard-on.

Our sex-only relationship sprang out of an evening of pizza and beer on the last day of American Jazz Masters class. I don't know where she came from—I'm pretty sure she wasn't a member of the class. It's possible she crashed the party—saw us crowded into the big booths in the corner of Pagliai's and just joined in. All I know is suddenly she was sitting across the table from me, drinking beer out of a pint glass and staring me down. I'm generally not one to avoid eye contact but this was so intense I found myself dropping my eyes, examining the bottom of my glass, pretending to belong to the conversation going on to my right. Whenever I looked across the table she had both headlights on me. It's hard to describe the look—it wasn't really lustful, more like she was just totally *into* me. Nobody had ever looked at me that way before.

"You want to go somewhere?" she said.

"Somewhere?" I replied stupidly. Maybe it was her eyes. They weren't made up at all, but they were still heavily lashed, and big, the size of a deer's. "You mean besides here?" I said.

"I was thinking ice cream," she said.

"Can you get ice cream this late? I don't think you can."

"Bet me," she said.

"Oh, I never gamble," I said. It came out more like a conversational ploy than I had intended. It was true that I didn't gamble; I didn't smoke either. So the hell what.

She pursed her lips and looked at the table, not out of any apparent shyness; more like a concentration strategy. I took the opportunity to try to sidle back into the conversation next door, but the discussions were too high context:

"They're not all like that."

"Most of them are, except for the younger ones, but they're worse because of the money."

"I actually believe the situation isn't that bad."

"Isn't that bad—you'd rather have a police state?"

And so on. At first I thought they were arguing about the elections, but when I offered up a comment I was met with a blank, polite silence. The next sentence made it clear, perhaps for my sake, that the conversation was actually a discussion of cigar import restrictions. When I glanced across the table at the girl, she showed no sign of having heard a word of what went on. She just stared, now silently.

"Do you have a car?" I asked.

She shook her head. "Motorcycle."

"Really? What kind? A Harley?"

She shook her head again, the exact same motion. "Moto Guzzi," she said.

"Is that a racing bike?"

And again the head shake. It was short—a quick side-to-side, like a pitcher shaking off a sign. I was beginning to like it.

"Too fat," she said. "They're supposed to be touring bikes, but you really don't want to go too far from home because they always break down and there just aren't that many places that work on them." She reached across the table, in front of everybody, and put her hand on mine.

I nodded sympathetically and, quite smoothly, slid my hand out from under hers. "I used to have a Norton," I said. "Same deal there." It was a lie; I never had a Norton. I never even had a Honda, and she knew it. Maybe because we both knew I was lying it seemed suddenly easier to talk.

"That was a nice fucking bike," I said. "I kept it in my living room, you know? I hung clothes on it and stuff." I thought this odd detail might steer us away from actual technical aspects of Nortons which might trip me up, like when they were built or what they actually looked like.

But she was nodding now. "Nortons were nice machines," she said. "Kind of like a T-Bird before they fucked them up."

"Exactly," I said. "That's a good way of describing them." Now we were just looking each other dead straight in the eye with no heavy weirdness. We were jelling big-time.

"What do you do in the winter," I asked, "to keep warm?"

"I walk," she said. "I ride the bus."

"The bus is warm," I agreed. "Too warm. You have to be careful not to fall asleep."

"People do all the time," she said. "All that fluorescent light and they still fall asleep."

Suddenly I knew something about her. I figured something out with only the tiniest amount of information to go on. I was very proud of myself.

"You're a driver, aren't you?" I said. "You drive the bus."

She nodded.

"You were driving when I fell asleep that time?" It was a few weeks back. She'd shaken me awake—gently, her hand on my shoulder—and dropped me off in front of my house.

"And you know where I live?"

She nodded again.

"I had a girlfriend once who was a letter carrier," I said. "She knew everything about me before I even met her."

"My uncle was a country clerk," she said. "He knew what everybody paid for their house. The church made him treasurer because he knew how to lean on people and get them to pay."

"Can you imagine being invisible?" I said. "You could know everything about somebody. Just follow them around everywhere they go, everything they do."

"I guarantee," she said, her beautiful eyes close up now and huge, "I *guarantee* there's ice cream open somewhere."

And that's how *that* got started. After we left the tavern

we never looked back, certainly never had ice cream. I rode on the back of her fat black Moto Guzzi. It was like holding on to a very fast tractor with your knees; that kind of powerful. The vibrations entered through my ass and I could still feel them all the way out on the tips of my fingers. We did a few turns on some Iowa farmland blacktop, then somehow found our way back, ending up at my place. It was a great ride.

Since the relationship was sex-only, I should describe the sex. A blast. A sensation. Weirdly emotional, like taking certain kinds of hallucinogenic mushrooms or watching a bad movie with a fever. Off the chart erections, loud breathing, dirty instructions missed and repeated. Sore lips, sorer genitalia, the occasional cramp in the calf or instep. Glasses of tepid water hurriedly downed, cold cereal spooned at all hours.

She was a nod-off sleeper. She didn't snore, but instead buzzed a little behind her nose. She grunted, farted. We were both out-facers, sleeping with our butts barely touching. She always woke before me, used my bathroom, and left without a word. By the time I opened my eyes the only sign she's been there at all was a messed-up throw rug by the bed and half as much toilet paper as when the day started. If we saw each other during the day we didn't speak; although once at the Coffee Haus I asked her if she was finished with her newspaper and she said she wasn't. On the bus it was even worse: no stolen glances in the rearview, no squeeze of the fingers when handing over the transfer. She didn't even pop the rear doors for me, the way she did for the elderly or infirm. Once I swear she passed my stop on purpose.

But still she showed up most nights, the Guzzi gurgling up the street, coughing a bit as she worked it into the narrow alley that ended under my window, then dying with a *hugg* sound, like an expiring whale. Her boots abused the back steps, then clattered across my kitchenette linoleum. She pushed open the pocket doors to my bedroom (my apartment was composed of the original kitchen and parlor of a narrow Victorian—my bedroom doors were massive, oak things that moved on hundred-year-old casters), then sat on the corner of my iron bedstead, creating one serious lean. By the time she had her clothes off I was a stiff little soldier, and we had nothing to talk about, even if we had wanted to.

t all blew up in my face because of the Norton lie. Not strictly— like I said, she knew it was bullshit from the start. But because I couldn't give it up. In fact, I expanded the whole Blue Norton thing into a kind of mega-lie. I worked that goddamn motorcycle into just about every nonconversation we had.

"Is the heat on?" she might say one night, facing away from me. "Does it seem hot to you?"

"Yeah," I'd say. "You know, I used to keep it a lot cooler when the bike was in the living room. Try to keep some of the oil out of the pan . . ."

Or her: "Is that rain? Is it really raining?"

Then me: "Tell me about it. Nortons are bad enough on *dry* pavement. Talk about slip-sliding away . . ."

Sometimes I inserted the old Norton into heavier conversations. Once when she asked me out of the blue about my parents' bust-up. Another time when she casually mentioned a bad sexual scene with an older man—a very bad experience, something that raised the hairs up under my ponytail. This didn't happen very often. But still every once in a while it did; then, enter the Blue Norton.

But she never called me on it, this lie. Well, once she did. Once and then it was over. It was about four in the morning and we were both eating cold chicken straight out of the refrigerator—and I mean literally the refrigerator door was *open*, and we sat on my cheap dinette stools in the cold light under the ice maker—when there was a sudden commotion from upstairs. It came out of the blue, no anticipatory stomping, quick footsteps, voices barely heard. This was simply a crash, followed—or was it preceded by?—a woman's scream. Then footsteps racing down the outside stairs. I padded to the window and slipped my fingers between the miniblinds. A woman ran off the bottom step and then up the alley, and I mean really ran. No shilly-shallying, no awkward lurching stumble. This one moved. She was down the alley and around the corner before the refrigerator door closed. It was very impressive.

"Wow," I said. "I wonder what that was all about."

She came up behind me in the dark there. A streetlight cut through the blinds and left slashes of amber across our bellies.

"You should go check," she said.

I dropped the blind. "What?"

"What do you mean, what? You should go up there and see if everything's okay."

"Forget it," I said. "I figure she just caught him screwing around. She walked in on something and couldn't deal."

"At four in the morning?"

"Of course at four in the morning. When do you think these things happen?"

"It could be an OD. It could be a heart attack. He might have attacked her and she ran."

"He's not the type," I said, although for all I knew, he could have been a sicko axe freak. I saw him once or twice a week at the mailboxes in the foyer. He was a typical jock, communications-major type. Had a big chest and one eyebrow that grew together in the middle. Probably played intramural basketball and drank stuff like Jägermeister or Jell-O shots at the underage bars. There were a thousand of him in town.

But she wasn't buying it.

"He's all right," I insisted. "Really. He used to borrow my bike."

"Your bike," she said.

I nodded. ". . . the Blue Norton." We both said it at the same time.

There was an awkward pause in the conversation.

"What are you afraid of?" she said finally.

"I'm not afraid of anything," I said. "Why don't *you* go up there?" I wanted to add, "You're the fucking commando," but I didn't.

"You know him," she said. "I don't."

"Barely."

"We can't just *stand* here," she said.

"Why not?"

She paused again, staring at me. "Just *go*," she said, suddenly softer. She was looking at me in the same way she had that night in Pagliai's—like there was something awfully damned important about my face right then. She reached over and squeezed my fingers. "Please," she said, in a voice I hardly recognized. I stared down at our joined hands like they were recently unearthed fossils. Even in that light her fingers were magnificent. "I'll put on my pants," I said. "Don't you think that would be a good idea?"

She squeezed my fingers again.

"Stay here," I said. "Make yourself at home."

What should I say about that night? The scene upstairs was all anticlimax. The girl had thrown a bowling ball through the glass of his back porch door, is all. I reached through the hole and let myself in. The ball had rolled a little ways into his kitchen. In one of the finger holes was a rolled-up note: *you bastard, rot in hell*, etc.—just as I had suspected. My neighbor was out at the time, though, and didn't come back until late the next morning. Thought it was all pretty funny. When I told him how fast she ran, he laughed.

"She told me she could run," he said. "Said she was some kind of track star in high school. Wouldn't shut up about it. I thought she was lying, you know, because she wasn't exactly skinny."

Something about that irked me, his smugness. "Girls gain weight when they first get to college," I said. "They call it the Freshman Fifteen."

"Yeah," he said. "I still thought she was lying, though."

But it was what happened when I went back downstairs that night; that was the clincher. She was standing in the kitchen all dressed, boots on and everything; jacket, the works.

"You're leaving?" I said. "Why?"

"I'm not," she said. "Just tell me what happened."

I told her and she didn't say anything for a while, like she was thinking something over. Then she said: "Wait a minute."

She went outside and fired up the fat old Guzzi, then began nuzzling the front tire right up against my back step. The headlight waggled a little bit, throwing bizarre planes and shadows all over the kitchen walls.

"How did you do it?" she said, loud over the Guzzi's heavy throb. "Did you have a ramp?"

"I don't know what you're talking about," I said. I held the door half open, half hiding behind it.

"Grab the screen," she said. "Don't let it clip the mirror." She gave her wrist a little twist, and the Guzzi humped itself up the first step like an advancing walrus. She worked the brake like an expert, and the fat bike hung there, tilted up, the

132

light now playing across my kitchen ceiling. Again her beautiful hands twitched; the Guzzi gurgled and popped, then hiked itself up the second step, its undercarriage groaning across the wooden lip. The front tire now rested just inches from the threshold.

"You're stuck," I shouted. "You should back it out."

She stared at me with those eyes. "You really want me to?"

"I don't know," I said. "We should talk about this."

"We already have," she said.

"We have?" It wasn't too late to close the door on her, too late to throw the dead bolt. Her front wheel was not quite on the threshold.

"This is a bad idea," I said. "Isn't it?"

She shrugged. "It's a gamble, that's for sure."

I looked over her head, at the mouth of the alley where only a few minutes before an entirely different girl had streaked away, running so fast it was magnificent to behold. She was here and then she was gone. But this one in front of me: she was one to be reckoned with. I could feel her vibration in the knob of the kitchen door and in the linoleum under my feet; the glass panes in my kitchen door rattled with the force of it.

"I'm just gonna goose it," she said. "Maybe you should stand back."

What could I do? I stood back.

kick in the head

When she was drinking she forgot to take her insulin at regular intervals. Her friends tried to look after her but what could we do? When I first met her she was staring at the wallpaper in a veterinarian's waiting room. I didn't see an animal anywhere near her, so I thought she might be sweating out an operation going on somewhere in the back. I was just there to hit up the veterinarian for some money for our Film Studies softball team.

"Are you okay?" I asked the woman. She was small and very pretty and well dressed but a little disheveled, like a bank teller or secretary who'd just had a bad shock.

She focused on me with some difficulty. "Listen to what?"

"Okay," I said. "Are you okay?"

She just stared. The receptionist's voice carried out through her Plexiglas window. "Celia," she said. "Are you low?"

Celia nodded slowly.

"Come on back," she said. "Come on back here and eat something."

The receptionist buzzed the door open and Celia disappeared behind it.

"Is she all right?" I said.

"She works here," the receptionist said. She looked at a clipboard and then put it down. "You're the softball guy?"

"It's really not much," I said. "Just enough for T-shirts and park fees."

The receptionist was uninterested. "The doctor will be with you in a minute."

Of course, Celia was the doctor. When she came back fifteen minutes later she was transformed. She'd put on a white sweater and was all brushed out and alert.

"Our big problem is too much business and then nothing," she explained. "It's hard as hell around here when all the little doggies are doing fine. I teach a couple of classes but it's not like real work."

"Where did you practice before?"

"NASA," she said.

"Excuse me?"

"God, I love your reactions," she said. "Very Little Rascals." She put her hand in a low pocket on her sweater and fished something out. "Here, hold out your hand."

She unrolled my index finger and smoothed it out a couple of times. I looked up at the receptionist but she was gone and the light was out back there. Celia unwrapped a small piece of metal, like a safety razor folded to a point.

"This is a lancet," she said. "I'm just going to get a baseline."

She was good; the jab felt like a cold flash and nothing more. She squeezed out a fat purple drop and smeared it across a little cardboard strip, holding the gun-metal blue lancet between two knuckles like a spent cigarette. She ran the cardboard through a little white calculator and then slid everything back into her sweater pocket.

"Let's get some ice cream," she said. "Then we'll see what you're really made of."

She forgot to test me after the ice cream. We went to her home on the river and flirted well past the point we needed to. She asked me to ignore the various elements of the house that pointed to a male presence—big stereo speakers, big-screen television, a recliner.

"Could we just pretend he was dead?" she asked. She brightened. "Oh, that face again. You sure you weren't a child actor?"

I didn't answer, I just attempted the face again.

"Well," she said. "It sure sucks when you do it that way."

There was a hot tub on the back deck. She loaned me a pair of swim shorts, faded blue with a net lining. The drawstring had disappeared on one side, and I worked to maneuver it back through to the eyelet. Finally she reached over and yanked it out completely.

"There's no diving board, sport," she said. "You'll be fine."

We drank Cuervo out of sake glasses, waiting for the tub to get hot or fizzy or something. She seemed to forget I was there every few minutes. Each time she re-noticed me she beamed.

"What kind of music do you kids listen to these days?" she said.

"Excuse me?" I said. "What year did you graduate high school?"

She told me. I was in grade school then, riding my bicycle, pissing in the bed.

"Do you like pornos?" she said. This time she laughed out loud at whatever my face did. "Wow," she said. "This is really fun."

"I'm a film student, remember? I don't like movies with no plot."

She got up and walked to the television cabinet filled with rows of black cassette cases. She pulled one out. "This is my all-time favorite," she said. "I don't even know the title."

She handed the case to me and I opened it. The label was typed out by hand. It was a Bette Midler movie that had just left town.

"The deceased," she said, "once wrote a screenplay and won a prize. Now any movie that's up for an Academy Award he gets on tape."

"I thought maybe he was a projectionist. You know, making illegal copies."

"He's a professor," she said. "But he acts like a teenager."

She nodded over to a picture on the TV stand. There was a little stab from the tequila in my stomach when I made the connection. "He's my professor," I said. "Except for the beard."

"He beats off all the time," she said, staring at the photograph. "He eats Cap'n Crunch. He makes noises when he eats that he isn't even aware of. He's afraid of children—I once saw him cross the street to avoid two kids with a basketball. He wears a retainer to bed. He goes into the bathroom to fart. He wrote me a poem for our wedding that absolutely sucked."

Sitting in his pale blue shorts I felt like a teenage girl, hearing this. "Why did you marry him?"

"Ask me a grownup question."

I stared at his picture. "He's in Toronto for two weeks," I said. "That's why we're not getting our papers back."

"Your papers," she said. "He grades them watching TV." She got up off the couch. "Do you want dinner?"

"Sure," I said. She seemed to have forgotten about the hot tub.

She brought some Tupperware out of the refrigerator. One had a jellied-looking roast and the other plain white spaghetti noodles. She got some plates down and tried to use two wooden spoons to ladle the cold noodles. She gave up and pulled them out with her fists. Her fingers left an oily smear on the microwave door.

"Are you low?" I asked.

"Well, aren't you suddenly the expert?" she said.

After dinner she tested me again. "Normal normal normal," she said. She put the lancet and the test strip down on the table.

"The time for making a pass has passed," she said.

"Oh," I said. Somehow along the way I had forgotten all about it. All I wanted was to watch her in action.

141

"The shorts might be missed," she said, pointing to my crotch. I went into the bathroom to change and when I came out she had opened up a little canvas bag. A vial and syringe sat next to her on top of the kitchen pass-through.

"I'm sorry about all this," she said without looking up at me. I stood for a second but she didn't move and didn't look up, so I left. I caught a ride on the campus bus back to my apartment.

Three days later she was arrested for drunk driving. They threw the book at her, which in that town meant forty-eight hours and a thousand dollars. But this was the Midwest and she got to keep her license.

I called her at the office and we met at the ice cream parlor.

"I'm glad you're out of there," I said. "Jail, I mean. I was worried about you."

She stared at me. "Oh, God," she said. "You're on that train, aren't you?"

"No," I said. "I'm not."

"You are, you are. I think I ought to know this look. I got married because of it."

"I'm not on any fucking train. My head is not in the clouds or anything like that. Can't I just call you without it having to mean anything?"

"Why?"

I couldn't answer, but she didn't leave me hanging for long.

"You know, that was no lie about NASA," she said. "We studied miniature pigs. Their respiration is almost identical to humans. They were going to go up in Skylab, then later on it was the Shuttle. We got shitcanned when Challenger blew up. Us and a lot of other people."

"Where did you study?"

"Ames," she said. "The government paid for every cent, thanks to our wonderful senator. I had a bacon endowment." Her ice cream had taken on an ignored look. Mine was gone.

"Hey, sport," she said. "Let's see that finger." Her lancet was out and the wrapper folded neatly back. I hadn't even seen her do it.

This time she was pissed. She looked at the calculator and then at me.

"You kids," she said. "Eat anything, do anything. If this was me the machine would be smoking."

"You know, maybe I'm a little on the train," I said.

She looked annoyed. "It's just that I have no respect for men right now," she said. "No offense, it just makes it kind of hard."

"Not for me," I said. "Respect is overrated."

She may have heard this, she may not have. She was back to staring at the white calculator. "This is incredible. Do you have a pulse?"

We left the ice cream store in her car and went golfing out by the interstate. It was like art should be, watching her swing a club. She couldn't hit the ball very far, but it was always a lovely arc, right down the middle. On the green she squatted like a catcher, her club grip up next to her ear. She was in in two every time. We only played nine and she had me by four strokes.

"You could smile," she said. "Be a good loser. It's kind of a sign of character."

"I am smiling," I said. "I'm just a little preoccupied." I was thinking that she was like this tiny Vietnamese girl I'd seen once, on drugs, get up on a table at a party and start go-go dancing. This was something you didn't see every day. Some of the worst-looking guys—gas company losers and bearded loggers—gathered tight around the table, like a Last Supper of goons. She was safe, I thought, as long as she stayed up there, but of course she came down. I protected her for a while—I think I even kissed her—but she ended up leaving with a guy with a Fu Manchu and a dirty cast on his wrist. I wondered about her for a little while until a couple of weeks later my roommate told me she'd become a stripper.

Celia slid her putter into her bag and zipped the top. "Gary taught me golf and then quit when I got good. How's that for a character quotient?"

I didn't answer. In the clubhouse we had Bloody Marys and I put my hand on her thigh, right where the big muscle splits in two and heads for the knee. She was tense; I felt like I had my hand on the back of a bobcat. I took it off.

"I better drive," I said.

"Nope," she said. "No way, José."

On the way back she rode off onto the shoulder and

mowed down three of the little white reflector posts. I felt them rattle along the floor under my feet.

I picked up my car at the ice cream store and followed her home. Back in her living room she played "All Along the Watchtower" over the big speakers.

"High school prom," she said. She started doing weird things with her hands, moving her feet on the carpet. "I made this dance up," she said. "I mean, me and my girlfriend." She did it some more. It was the kind of dancing you'd see in a documentary.

"I want to see you shoot up," I said. She didn't even stop dancing.

"Did you hear me?" I said.

"No."

"No you didn't hear me or no I can't watch?"

She said something but I couldn't hear it over the raspy guitar. It had started to weave back and forth between the speakers, one side to the other.

The song ended and she crossed over and sat down on my lap. She was very drunk. "Do the thing with your face," she said. "I love that thing."

"At least show me the needle," I said.

She pursed her lips. "Noooo," she said. Her pupils were the size of blazer buttons and her breath was heavy and thick with something like wine.

I put my hands on her hips, just where they tucked in beneath her ribs. She made a squirmy little gyration on my lap and I untucked her shirt for her.

"Should you have something to eat?" I asked, my fingers on her bottom blouse button. She shrugged and did another little wiggle.

"Seriously," I said, unbuttoning my way from the bottom to the top. I separated the sides of her blouse. The skin of her belly was very white and her bra was an odd tan color. She shivered, then swayed a little. I took my hands off her shirt.

"Now I'm worried," I said. "I really don't know what to do here."

She ignored me. The music had changed, now it sounded like Dean Martin, and she crooned along, tilting her head from side to side. "My life is going to be beeeeyootiful," she sang. Then her eyes went back in her head and she was down on the floor before I could get hold of her.

I dialed 911. "Ain't that a kick in the head?" sang Dean Martin.

Ketoacidosis isn't as bad as it sounds. Her husband didn't even find out about it himself until six months later, when he was having a drink with one of the paramedics at a sports bar. But by then it hardly mattered.

After the paramedics were done fixing her up, they tried to load her into the ambulance but she refused to go. They called the receptionist—whose name was Rachel—and she came over to spend the night. I passed her in the driveway. She was wearing a raincoat and carrying a bag of crocheting.

"She's all right," I said. "When I told them she was a diabetic they knew just what to do."

She looked at me like I was a tick. I caught her elbow as she passed.

"Can I talk to you a minute?" I said. She didn't say no so I kept talking. "She was lying there going on and on about Skylab," I said. "Does she do that a lot?"

The receptionist took a long breath and nodded. "Skylab, space shuttles, Houston. I heard it all." She put her bag down. "She used to be better, when she first came here. She would get mad, she would cry sometimes, but not this up and down. Not this up and down all the time." She looked like she wanted to say more but she just picked up her bag. "You should do yourself a favor and stick to girls your own age."

I got into my car and passed a local cop in his square Dodge at the mouth of her street, watching for speeders down the hill there, at least that's what I thought. He pulled me over not a hundred yards past.

He walked up with his flashlight held next to his ear. "That's a Stop sign back there," he said.

"I know," I said. "You mean I didn't stop?"

"Can you turn the music down, please?"

I did and he switched the flashlight to his other hand. "Driver's license, please," he said. When I handed it to him he shined the flashlight on it. After a moment he raised his eyes from the card. "Been drinking tonight, Andrew?" he said.

"I was earlier," I said. "But there was a little excitement

and an ambulance and I don't think I can feel a thing any-more."

He handed me back my license. "What was that all about?"

"My friend didn't take her medicine and she sort of passed out."

"Yeah, well, I know all about your friend," he said, look-ing up at the house. "I tagged her last week. She's a train wreck waiting to happen."

"She's having trouble at work," I said.

He leaned down, his fat palm on the rubber window sill next to my ear. He had a prickly moustache that poked out like tiny spines from his upper lip. He wasn't much older than me.

"So what's the deal with her?" he said. "She was mad as hell when I picked her up, then all of a sudden she starts cry-ing like a baby. The matron almost sent her over to Mercy Hospital. Thought she might do something stupid."

"Oh, I don't know," I said.

"Look," he said, "my business begins and ends with this ticket book here. But if you want some friendly advice I'd tell you to steer clear."

"Yeah," I said. "I know what you mean." The whole time he kept the flashlight beam drifting around the interior of the car. Some friend.

He hung around for another few seconds. "Anyway," he said, stepping away from the door. "I'd adjust those headlights before inspection."

"Excuse me?"

"Your headlights. They're pointed too high. They're an obstruction."

"I'll take care of it," I said.

I talked to her on the phone the next day.

"What did you do to me when I was out?" she said. "Should I be worried?"

"*I* was worried," I said. "I didn't sleep all night."

"You? When I woke up Rachel was sitting there asleep with her mouth open and her fucking knitting everyplace."

"Listen," I said. "I don't care about your husband anymore. I want to officially start something going here."

"You could have fooled me," she said, but her voice was gentle. "Tell me something. Did you used to take home strays when you were a kid?"

"You're not a stray," I said.

"No," she said, "I'm not."

"Look, I can tell you lots of good things about you. Lots of reasons to feel like this."

"I'm sure you can. Listen," she said. "He took someone with him up there to Canada, all right? Comprende? Make sense now?"

"Are you sure?"

"Positive. She's probably in your stupid class. Wants to be Francis Ford Coppola or make rock videos or something."

In a second I pictured her; the blonde girl from Brooklyn with the dreadlocks. It was so obvious.

"I know who it is," I said. "I'm sure it doesn't mean any-thing," I said.

"Does it ever?"

"Of course it does sometimes," I said.

"I wonder, sport." I could hear the music from her big fucking stereo. It sounded like the Dean Martin again.

"Well, I'm waiting," she said finally.

"For what?"

"All the things," she said. "All the things that are so great about me."

She didn't wait long. She hung up while I was still think-ing.

A couple of days later she plowed into the side of a corner ranch in the middle of the night. Nobody was hurt except for a dog which had been sleeping on the porch and was trapped by a fallen post. The rescue of the trapped dog made it onto the local news, along with garishly lit shots of Celia stagger-ing around the lawn, holding one shoe in her hand like a high-ball. The woman on the local news took it easy on her and said that she'd had some medication problems, and for some reason she wasn't arrested.

I read up on diabetes in the library. It had been a death sentence before injectable insulin. Besides the physical angle it also had psychological effects; mood swings, depression, ir-ritability, euphoria. It was of supreme importance to maintain a steady blood-glucose level. With constant monitoring and lots of support, diabetics could maintain a fairly normal life. I put the book down on the library table and used the pay phone.

She didn't answer. I left a message on her machine that I'm sure she was standing there listening to.

"I can't stop thinking about you," I said. "Pick up." When she picked up I was going to tell her what I had thought about a few days before, about all of the things that were so great about her. But she didn't pick up. I went home and drank all the beer in my refrigerator and then drove to her house, but I didn't dare try to make it past the cop at the mouth of her street. He was sitting there, pretending to be watching the road again. But I knew what he was watching for. I didn't know his name or where he was from or even if he was married, but I knew that. I called her again from a pay phone.

"Pick up," I said. "It's me." But she didn't. I took a breath and started to launch into all the things I'd memorized, but I'd waited too long and the machine cut me off.

The very next night someone ran over a thirteen-year-old boy coming home from Chess Club on his bike. Luckily, the kid he was riding with was a highly decorated Boy Scout and saved his life by pressing on some artery until the ambulance came, but the boy still lost the arm and was in a coma.

The driver didn't even slow down. I knew it was her. When I passed the mouth of her street, the young cop was gone.

Her rental car was in the garage, the front end hidden in blackness. She was out back in the hot tub, her stereo playing loud. She was dancing and floating at the same time, her eyes closed. Her head was normal but the rest of her dangled underwater like flapping blue laundry. The music was something old and slow—not Dean Martin. Dean Martin would have been wildly inappropriate under the circumstances.

I sat up on the wooden deck and waited for the song to end. When it did, she spoke first.

"I've got some serious problems, Andrew," she said.

"I know. I saw it on the news."

She opened her eyes. "I looked terrible. Like a drunken hooker. Think about your mother seeing you with someone like that."

"Did you run over someone tonight? If you did, it doesn't matter to me."

She slid her feet underneath her and raised out of the water a little. She looked a little shocked; her face was almost like that of a young girl.

"Is this the way you sweet-talk someone?" she said. "Is this the real you?"

"Maybe I'm different than you think," I said.

I handed her a towel and she clambered over the side of the hot tub and walked inside, her feet slapping against the boards of the deck.

"Maybe," she said.

Inside she went to a large oak desk and opened a drawer. She pulled out a handful of white plastic pouches, a vial, and some alcohol. She pulled a syringe from one of the pouches and carried it and the vial over to the kitchen pass-through, where the tall stools were. She was quick; she rolled the vial between her fingers, stuck the needle in, tapped it, and injected the insulin into the her thigh like she might have been putting down a collie. The entire room smelled of alcohol. She sat on the bar stool and put her head in her arms. Her wet hair fell on either side of her face. Water from the hot tub dripped from her toes. She stayed there with her head in her arms and didn't move, even when I crossed the room and stood next to her.

"There, there," I said, stroking one of her forearms with my fingertips. "Everything's going to be fine." After a minute I gathered her up and carried her into her bedroom. It was dark in there, with just the muddy blue light from the hot tub crawling around the ceiling. The music had changed on its own to the Dean Martin. As I put her down I told her all the things about her that I had come up with over the last few days, all the things that made her so great. She smiled with her eyes closed at every one of them.

". . . and your life," I told her right in time with the music, "is going to be beautiful." It wasn't a lie—it was true right then, before the insulin worked its way through her, dissolving the poisonous sugar out of her blood. Before the sun came up and illuminated the front of her garage and the cop reappeared at the mouth of her street. Before her husband came back. Before she remembered what we were all really like.

american

a*r*ms

t was 1966 at the American Arms in Wiesbaden that Christopher Bergman got his first haircut by himself; no father or mother to supervise, just the seven-year-old boy and the barber. The hotel was full of U.S. Air Force personnel—some arriving, some leaving—and it seemed he was the only person in the hotel without a destination any more remote than the barber's chair. He arrived ten minutes early and sat in one of the chipped wooden seats by the window overlooking the dirty marble lobby. The barber was running a comb through a teenager's hair, every few strokes dipping the comb in a glass of blue fluid. The barber used both hands; his free hand shadowed the hand working the comb, adding little fingertip pats. The teenager twitched his nose but otherwise sat still, staring at the wall across the room, while the barber played his head like a harp.

Christopher Bergman picked up a magazine from the square end table and let it fall open on his lap to a page of its own choosing. It revealed an ad, entirely in German, for hair creme. He wondered if it was a special magazine just for barbershops, made to open only to hair creme ads. He flipped a few pages and stopped on one with a naked woman, looking surprised, sitting with her legs crossed on a thick white rug, her elbow on one knee. Her expression was that of a woman caught doing something against the rules by someone she liked. He flipped quickly past the photograph to another hair creme ad. After a moment he began meticulously turning the pages at an even rate, back and forth past the page with the naked woman. He tried to give the page with the naked woman equally as much attention as the hair creme ads, but found that it was hard to look at her for more than a second or two. In fact, the hair creme ads were a welcome respite from the photograph of the naked woman, and soon he stopped flipping back and forth at all and tried to decipher the German words in a motorcycle ad. He found the word that he thought meant fast and the one that must have meant powerful and another that probably meant smooth or inexpensive or maybe new. He never found the one that meant motorcycle.

When the teenager hopped down from the chair and paid the barber, Christopher noticed with satisfaction that he failed to tip. Christopher had the money for his tip in a separate pocket from the other money, the dollar-fifty for the cost of the haircut. He had practiced the way he would give the tip to the barber: he had decided on "There you are" over "This is yours" or "This is for you." If the barber had been American he might have gone with "There you go," but he was afraid that it might be misconstrued somehow, as if he were asking the barber to leave his own country. His father had made it clear that even though the tip looked like very little money, it was important not to forget to give it and that it was actually quite a good amount when converted into German *pfennig*. His father didn't tell him what to say when he handed over the fifty cents; Christopher wished he had but he didn't have the nerve to ask him.

When the teenager had finished paying, Chris stood up from his chair, but just as quickly the barber held up his hand. In the door, brushing past the teenager, walked an officer and a woman. It was not an American officer, and it was not an American woman. The barber spoke to the officer in German and the officer took off his jacket and loosened his tie. He sat down in the barber chair and leaned forward while the barber slipped a tissue inside his shirt collar, then settled a white cover over his shoulders like a cape. He twisted the tissue and adjusted the cape and smoothed it over the officer's lap. When the barber was done, the officer leaned forward and raised one knee under the cape, crossing his legs. He removed his eyeglasses with a partially covered arm and rested them on the upraised crown of his knee, the stems hanging down on either side. The officer pinched the bridge of his nose, grimacing and working the loose skin up and down a few times, then let his hands fall to the arms of the chair. The barber made one final smooth of the cape to fit the new position of the officer's arms, then picked up his scissors and began snipping the air next to the officer's left ear. Christopher sat back down in his seat.

The woman had chosen a seat close to Christopher, closer than she need have. He looked at her. She was not old and not

159

young. She was not pretty and not ugly, not smiling and not frowning. She had a small round cap and cold blond hair with a stiff-looking bend around the back of the ears. She had frosted lips and small chips of black on her bottom eyelashes. She was gazing down at Christopher, her expression curious and her eyes flitting back and forth between his face and his lap. Christopher sent her the neutral expression that he had used in the past on his mother's friends from the Officers' Wives Club when he took their coats upstairs to his parents' bed. He wasn't sure what this neutral expression really looked like; all he knew was that everyone found it acceptable. The women who came in the door smiling continued smiling, the ones that came in looking anxious continued looking anxious, and the ones that came in looking grim and used up didn't really bother to look at him at all. In the first few weeks after his mother died, the expression had become extraordinarily useful; since then he had needed it only sporadically.

But this perfectly neutral expression was lost instantly when he looked down and saw that the magazine on his lap had fallen open to the page with the surprised naked woman sitting cross-legged on the thick white carpet. His face filled with heat and seemed to float a centimeter or so in front of its normal spot close to his ears. He moved his hand away from the center fold of the magazine, and, with agonizing slowness, a sizable clump of pages flopped over, covering the woman and revealing once again the original hair creme ad.

He peered intently at the page and counted to fifty. Then he closed the magazine and placed it back on the table next to him. Only when he was sure it wasn't going to slide off the table and onto the floor (exposing God knows what) did he look up at the officer's woman. When he saw her face, the tiny uncut hairs on the back of his neck rippled, then rippled again. She sat on the seat next to him in the barbershop with her legs crossed, looking somehow delightedly surprised, as if she had just caught someone doing something against the rules—someone she liked.

"And so yes," she said, her "s" hard and German. "You are married?"

"No," Christopher said. "I'm too young."

She beamed at him in a way that made him believe it was fake. "You are a bad boy, then," she said. "Making me laugh."

"You're not laughing."

"Bad boy," she repeated. "Making me laugh."

The barber said something in German to the officer and from the barber chair the officer said something in German to the woman. She ignored him. She uncrossed her legs and leaned a bit closer to Christopher, as if sharing a secret. He leaned away.

"Come to home," she said. "Come with me to home to marry, yes?"

"I don't understand German," Christopher said. He wished the woman wouldn't speak to him. He was afraid the barber didn't like it; a boy speaking to an important officer's wife.

"*Fuh, cherman,*" she said, her lips pursed as if she had tasted something sour. "You speak to me with French, yes?"

The officer said something else and the woman lowered her voice and her smile disappeared. "*Parlez-vous français? No?*"

The barber glared at them, threw his scissors down on the counter with a clatter, and picked up a fat pair of clippers. He snapped his thumb and the clippers began to whine. When he pressed them to the officer's head they warbled angrily. The officer protested in German and the barber eased up.

"Your mother is living, yes?" the officer's wife said. "Living in hotel?"

"Yes," he said. "I mean, no."

"Oh, she is at home in United States, yes?"

"Yes." Christopher thought how best to make himself understood, how best to lie to the woman. "She packs the house," he said. "She comes to Germany soon." He was afraid she was playing nice only to inform on him about the magazine. Officers' wives did such things for each other. He prayed his father didn't walk into the lobby at that moment and decide to speak to him. A father was as good as a mother for something like that.

But now the woman was silent. Christopher watched her throat as she breathed. Her smile was gone; she seemed, if anything, suddenly all business.

Finally she spoke. "Your father to see me, yes?" She pronounced it "fozzer."

Christopher's throat constricted. "My father is not at home," he said. It was all he could think of.

He was distracted by loud laughter from the barber's

chair. The officer had his hand on the forearm of the barber; the clippers whined futilely in the air next to his head while the barber listened with pursed lips to the officer's story. When the officer finished his laughter, the barber spun him in his chair and bore down on the back of his neck with determination, coercing the officer's chin down to his chest. The officer breathed heavily through his nose but was otherwise silent.

When Christopher turned back to the woman, she was watching him even more intently than before. He felt as though she had moved slightly closer to him.

"I try to being nice to you," she said. "You are making difficult, yes."

"Sorry." He realized that for some time he had not been concentrating on keeping his expression neutral. That was what was causing this scene to go wrong, to get out of hand. He wished he could take the woman's coat and lay it on a bed somewhere, put ice cubes in a glass for her, return her coat on demand; these things he could still pull off with his eyes closed, even in German. He wondered what would happen if he returned to their room with his hair uncut, what his father would do. He had no idea, he could not imagine it.

This was the exact moment when Christopher's father walked into the barbershop; he appeared, and as soon as Christopher saw him he realized that he had known all along he would be there. His father stopped near the doorway, noticed Christopher in the chair, saw the German officer with the barber, then lifted his wrist and looked at his watch. The barber noticed him and the clippers went silent. The German officer had his eyes closed; he opened them when the barber unceremoniously dropped the barber chair six inches and yanked the tissue from around his neck. At the same time the German officer's wife stood up and approached Christopher's father. All four of them met at the barber's chair; Christopher stayed in his seat.

The officer said something in German and settled back in his chair, his mouth tight. The barber spoke to him curtly; the woman, holding her purse in front of her, repeated it. Christopher's father said nothing. The German officer crossed his arms in front of him, over the white cape, and set his jaw tighter yet. Nothing happened for a moment, then the woman turned to the barber and spoke to him. The barber's face flushed. He raised his hand and struck the woman on the face; it was so fast it might not have happened at all, except that the woman's hat fell to the floor, landing next to serrated snips of her husband's trimmed hair. Christopher's father froze with his mouth slightly open in the beginnings of a protest. The barber spoke quickly to Christopher's father, then turned on his heel and walked through a curtain in the rear of the shop. The German officer and his wife stared at each other without moving; the woman did not even raise a hand to her cheek the way people did on television when they were slapped in the face.

After a moment Christopher's father crossed over to Christopher and stood before him. Christopher began to get out of the seat, but his father held up his hand.

"Go ahead and get in the chair as soon as these people leave," he said. "The barber will be back in a few minutes." His father looked around and then reached over and picked up the German magazine from the table and handed it to Christopher. "Here, see what you can make of this," he said. "I'll see you at six in the restaurant. Don't watch too much television."

"I don't understand any of it, it's all in the wrong language," Christopher said. "Can't I come with you?" The magazine lay unopened in his lap.

Christopher's father seemed surprised. They looked at each other for a long time until his father finally dropped his eyes. "I'm sorry, sport," he said. He walked to the door, stepping back to let the German officer and the woman out first.

When he was finished, the barber had cut Christopher's narrow sideburns unevenly and nicked his ear with the fat clippers, drawing blood. Christopher paid for the haircut in tears, forgot his jacket on the coat rack, and, despite his careful planning, failed to tip. He spent the rest of the afternoon hanging around the lobby shrugging irritably from the sharp hairs trapped in the fabric of his shirt, afraid to go back in and claim his jacket.

The teenager from the barbershop confided to him later in the afternoon that the officer was actually a chauffeur, the woman a prostitute, and the barber a former SS colonel who had once run a concentration camp and had only just gotten out of prison. The teenager said that it was common knowledge the hotel was full of Russian spies from East Berlin. He offered to give Bergman his old comic books when he was transferred out, which was any day now. The teenager was from Fairchild Air Force Base, near Spokane, and he was determined to get out of Germany and back home in time to graduate from an American high school. He confided to Bergman that he had packed his suitcase three days earlier, even though his father was still awaiting his final transfer orders; every day the teenager sat in his hotel room hoping to get the news they were going home, and every evening he was disappointed.

funny
cars

We're on our way out of town to see Garcia about some parts for Bobby's Camaro when the muffler falls off. I hear the sudden roar when it lets go and the *thunk* as it tumbles under the rear end. Behind us it skids to a stop and spins slowly for a second, the twisted pipe pointing up into the air like a jagged finger saying *Come along*. Bobby rubs the back of his head with his knuckles and cusses, and when he takes the spur to Garcia's he brings both hands to the top of the steering wheel and jerks it a quarter-turn to the right. The Camaro sits low and takes the turn without sway, like a door swinging on a hinge. When Garcia's road turns to gravel beneath us, the wheel wells begin to ping and behind us a plume of dust angles off the road and onto the soybeans, already powdered with gray on either side of the road. The air in the car starts to coat the back of my throat.

Up ahead Garcia's barn comes into sight, circled by junked and rusty cars. Garcia is sitting out on his front porch holding an ice tea. Over his T-shirt he wears a brace made of steel bars and plastic shoulder pads that holds his broken neck in place; it's connected to a plastic chin cup and a metal ring that circles his forehead. According to Bobby the headband is screwed into his skull in four places: two in front, two in back. It's his first day out of the hospital. Just three weeks ago Garcia rolled his Mach 1 four times, breaking his neck and killing Stacey Stehle, who was in the passenger seat, and nearly killing her twin sister Connie, in back. Five years before that, Garcia split his Barracuda on a power pole, killing two other people I hadn't heard of. He walked away from that one—Bobby says he leads a charmed life.

Bobby's older brother Russ hadn't been so lucky. When Bobby was ten, Russ was out on leave from Vietnam and was killed in a car crash in Germany. The Camaro had belonged to Russ, originally, and when Bobby's other brother was sent straight out of the Navy to Leavenworth, his parents gave it to Bobby for his birthday. It's a gutless Camaro, as Chevys go, and as much as Bobby wishes it was a muscle car, it never quite makes it. It burns oil and goes through a new clutch every six months. Bobby keeps adding a new part here and a new part there, but nothing seems to help.

We pull in and stop behind a rusty trailer with Garcia's fat-tired LeMans sitting on it, the one he races on weekends on the dirt track at Millstadt, bright yellow and covered with car-parts stickers and the number 23. Through the hole where the back window should be I can see the leather web of the driver's harness hanging from the ceiling. We slam our doors and Garcia lifts himself off his chair using his arms, his back held perfectly straight. Beneath the brace his shoulders bulge. He picks up a yardstick that is leaning against the porch rail and takes the three steps down from his porch carefully.

Bobby meets him about halfway up the brown lawn. "Hey, buddy," he says. "How's it going?"

Garcia takes a second or two. "All right," he says. "I'm making it." He turns his whole trunk and looks at the road we came in on. "Look at the fucking dust," he says. "You make me sneeze and I'll kick your ass, man. A sneeze could kill me."

Bobby acts like he didn't hear. "Remember you said you had those lifters for sale? That time in the park?"

Garcia nods with his eyes over at the trailer. "Back of the car."

We walk over to the trailer, Garcia behind us. The doors to the LeMans are welded shut, so Bobby climbs up onto the trailer and leans in through the open window. Being six-seven, I can see into it from where I stand. Where the back-seat should be there's a pile of tools and rags and a few empty cans. The car smells like it's been rained in.

"Nice rig," I tell Garcia.

He snorts. "Fuck it," he says. He walks around to the front, dragging his fingers on the trailer. "I'm selling it. Selling all this shit."

I follow along a little behind him. "You going to quit racing now, huh?"

"Hell, no," he says. He bends his trunk back and looks up at me. "I'm going pro-stock. Straight lines, man, no more of these dirt tracks." He stops and leans carefully against the trailer. He works his jaw against the cup under his chin. The cup makes his voice sound nasal and lippy. "Then funnies, then maybe top fuel, if I get a decent sponsor. There all you

171

got to worry about is fire. Five, six seconds, bam, it's over, and you pick up your check."

Bobby jumps down from the trailer with a small blue box in his hand. "How much?"

Garcia works his jaw around some more. "Twenty," he says.

Bobby puts on a pained expression. "I only brought ten bucks with me, and now I got to get a new muffler." He scratches at the gravel in the driveway with his heel.

"I got a muffler for that Chevy. Brand new, almost. You can have 'em both for thirty."

Bobby scratches at the gravel some more and bites his lip. "Tell you what," he says. "I'll give you the ten for the muffler now, and I'll come back for the lifters." Before Garcia can answer he turns and walks back to the LeMans, leans up, and pushes the blue box through the window. He walks back up to us and Garcia scowls at him as much as he can in his head rig. He rotates his shoulders toward the barn.

"In there on the right. Take the one with the short pipe, it came off a Chevelle."

Bobby walks off and Garcia and I stand out in the late afternoon sun without talking. Garcia takes the yardstick and runs it under the armpit of the shoulder harness and pushes it in short strokes between his shoulder blades. His eyebrows and nose twitch like a dog's when he scratches, and it's all I can do not to smile.

After a second he seems to notice me again. "You race?" he says. He asks like he's never seen me before, never flicked cigarette butts at me in the park, called me names like Too-Tall and Shit-for-Brains.

"I don't have a car," I say. There's no way I'm going to tell him I don't even have a driver's license. He scrunches up his face and I can tell it's his way of shaking his head now that he can't.

"Smart. Cars are a pain," he says. "Royal pain." He swings his trunk around slightly, waving at the expanse of his yard. "All these and I don't even got one that runs anymore."

When Bobby returns he holds out the ten, tucking the muffler under his other arm. "Be back for the lifters in a week or so," he says.

When Garcia holds out his hand to take the bill, his whole torso leans back to compensate for the weight of his arm. "Watch the dust when you leave," he says, already walking back to the porch.

In the car, Bobby leans forward and unbuttons his shirt and onto the floor roll a half-dozen stainless steel cylinders, making dull clacking sounds against each other. I have no idea where in an engine they might go. He fires up the motor, and when we get to the end of Garcia's road, just where the gravel ends, he slows and then punches the gas. The car roars and slips sideways, and from the back a cloud bunches up to blow back toward Garcia's porch.

I look at Bobby and he shrugs. "Screw him," Bobby says. "What's he going to do? Let's face it, one pop to the head and he's Jell-O, and he knows it."

I consider Garcia's size, the pressurized strength in his

arms, the one blow to the neck turning it all into so much wasted meat. It's a strange feeling to feel sorry for Garcia—Garcia who used to terrorize the smaller kids in high school, Garcia who walked away from half a burning car—and to see the fear in his eyes when he talked about dust. Hell, I think to myself, a good laugh would probably kill him, too.

t the park, as the sun goes away, we run into Paula Cates sitting on one of the picnic tables. Tonight her dark hair looks a little rattier than usual and her jean jacket gives off a musty dope smell. She's smoking a cigarette, and a bottle of beer rests between her feet, hidden from the road.

"Hey," she says to Bobby. "Mr. Cool." She straightens up a little, and when she smiles she looks a little better, even though you can see her yellow front tooth. "And the Big Man," she says, looking at me. I feel a stupid smile go on my face, but I can't help it. She watches me for a second, and her face keeps the smile longer than it usually does. She knows that she makes me nervous, but she never takes advantage of it. She's the only one who calls me Stretch that I don't mind; she never smirks when she says it. She has a wide mouth—too wide, some people might say—that curves around under her cheeks, and when she laughs loud it opens and splits her face like a tree trunk that's being felled. She's not pretty but she has a certain kind of spirit that you never see in people with small features, baby mouths and little noses, and I've always liked the way her face fit her.

Years before, when they closed St. Mark's and Bobby and Paula and all the rest of the Catholic kids from the south side of town had to come to our school, Paula had sat next to me in Earth Studies, and I'd let her use my answers. After class I'd watch her when she'd walk out the gate and get into some high-school guy's growling car and speed off. One of those cars had been Garcia's, the first one he crashed, years ago, the crash he'd walked away from. Another one had been the black Camaro we just got out of, when Bobby's brother Russ had been alive. The two of them had been serious, even though when he left she was only fifteen or so.

"Hey, Cates," Bobby says, "how goes the Death Watch?"

Paula shakes her head. The Death Watch thing comes from the week before, when we'd run into her getting out of some guy from Belleville's GTO, wearing her black jeans and this little fur-necked short jacket. She saw us hanging out and came over and we went to the park and she got us high. She was drunk and kept running her hand up and down Bobby's arm. It made Bobby nervous and he made up some excuse and left, so Paula and I sat in the bleachers at the A-league diamond and drank some Mogen David. That was about two weeks after Stacey Stehle had been killed in Garcia's wreck, and it was all Paula could talk about.

It seems the Stehle sisters' parents and family had all been standing around in the emergency-room hall that night weeping when in walked drunk Paula, all decked out in her torn jeans and eye makeup and ratty hair, who had never said five words to the Stehle sisters in her life. She'd just heard about the accident from some people at a tavern and had gone straight to the hospital to check it out.

"It was weird," she'd said, pulling on the bottle. "I mean, I heard about it and I just *had* to be there. I just *had* to see it. I mean, shit, they had been in *my* car. So I hung around until the doctors threw me out, and came back the next day, and the day after, and I was even there all day today, waiting for her to wake up."

Paula handed me the bottle and looked around the in-field, shaking her head. "I mean, her folks thought I was some friend they hadn't met, you know? They've been holding my hand and hugging me and buying me lunch at the goddamn cafeteria all week long." She plucked at the arm of her coat. "I mean, look at me—to think these people would believe someone like me would be caught dead hanging around with that tight-ass."

"So what happens when she wakes up?" I asked her.

"I don't know, Stretch," she said, "I'm just waiting on that one. Maybe she'll have amnesia, maybe she'll think I'm her goddamn sister." That had made her laugh, a short, shallow laugh. "That would be classic, now, wouldn't it?" She laughed again. "Can you imagine?"

But that was last week, and now Paula shakes her head. The Death Watch is over.

"She woke up, huh?" I say.

"Woke up on Wednesday, went home Thursday. They hired a nurse to sit with her all day. They say she's got the mind of a three-year-old—wets the bed and everything. They don't know if it's the medication or brain damage or what." Paula drags on her cigarette and flicks the ash onto the grass. She shakes her hair and sighs. "I don't know, man, they won't even let me in the house."

"But they thought you were best friends."

"Yeah, well," she says, "I guess someone gave them the scoop. I went over to the house that same day they took her home, and again yesterday, and they wouldn't even let me in the door."

"They didn't say anything?"

"They said they'd have me over for dinner in a month or two, for Christ's sake."

"Good," Bobby says. I see that his face has gotten a little red and his jaw is tight. "She's better off. Just leave the girl alone, why don't you."

Paula looks up, surprised. "Oh, come on, Kessick." Her mouth is hanging a little open and her eyes are narrow and she looks at him like this for a moment. "Anyway, you're the one that brought it up."

"Yeah," he says, his voice a little thin, "maybe I'm just sick of hearing about people getting wiped out in car crashes all the time." He gets up from the table and pushes his hands into the pockets of his jacket, and starts kicking the back of his heel into the sod. Paula and I are silent. I know he's thinking of his brother getting killed on the Autobahn and I wonder if Paula's made the connection. After all, she'd gone out with Russ, and she'd been at the wake, higher than usual. She'd had to walk out in the middle and be sick in the bathroom. On top of all that, Bobby always had a thing for the Stehle sisters, either one of them. They were out of his league, and he knew it; everybody did.

Bobby stops kicking and looks at Paula. "You got a problem with that?"

"No, I got no problem with that, but I can't say I really give a shit. I mean, nobody told them people to drive around drunk like they did, running into poles and shit."

"Yeah?" Bobby says. "Then why hang out in the hospital for a week? Taking a survey?"

"I was *interested*," Paula says. Her eyes narrow and her lip sticks out. "Understand? At least I cared."

"I thought you just said you didn't care," Bobby says. "Get your story straight. Fact is, you're just a vampire. These were nice girls and you should have just stayed out of it."

"Yeah, nice," Paula says. She turns the bottle over and drains the foam in the bottom out onto the grass. Her face is calm, but I see her teeth clench, just a little. After a second she looks up. "You know, Kessick," she says, "what you don't know would fill a book." She holds the empty bottle by the neck and tosses it into the grass under the table. "Let me tell you something about our little cheerleader friend you'll really like."

"Hey," Bobby says, "hey. Don't waste my time."

"Fuck you, Kessick," she says, and turns to me, "I'm talking to Stretch." She takes a drag from her cigarette and flicks it into grass at Bobby's feet. It sizzles when it hits the dew.

Without anything in her hands now, she pulls her feet up under and sits on the edge of the table cross-legged.

"Remember I said they wouldn't let me into the house anymore?" I nodded. "Well, the last three days I've been hanging out in that field across the street, watching. And guess what I see the last three nights at nine o'clock on the nose?"

"Don't tell me," Bobby says, "a ghost. You see Stacey Stehle come riding by in her car, laughing and carrying on."

"Close," Paula says. She puts a hand on my knee. "Listen up, Stretch, you'll like this. The last three nights at nine o'clock old Connie gets up in her bedroom window buck naked and just stands there, staring out at the street until it gets dark."

"*What?*" Bobby says, walking around behind me so he's in front of Paula. "Come *on* with this. She just stands there with no clothes on, staring out the window? That's a load of crap."

"Why?" I say. "What's she looking at?"

Paula laughs. "Hell if I know. Maybe she's looking for Stacey." She looks at Bobby. "Maybe Stacey *is* driving down that street, but Connie's the only one can see her."

"Oh, that's *bullshit*," Bobby says, almost spitting the words. "That's nothing but *bullshit*."

Paula straightens out her legs, resting her feet back on the bench, and leans back on her elbows. "Relax, Kessick," she says. She is smiling. "You'll give yourself a hernia or something. She ain't looking for you, so don't get so worked up." She smiles even wider without turning her head.

"Besides, stud, it's about a quarter to nine right now, and the sun's just about down. If you two are going to make it," she says, turning and looking him in the eye, "you better fire up that piece of shit you call a car and get the hell out there."

Bobby stands there, working his jaw. "It's bullshit," he says again, but he's already walking toward the car.

When we pull away I look back and see Paula on the bench in the long shadows, lighting another cigarette. The flare of the match shows her face for a second, and I can see she is no longer smiling. She frowns the same way Garcia did when we drove away from his place, filling the air with engine noise and dirt.

There's a grid of paved streets out north of the town, streets carved into old cornfields with light poles that flicker on and off all night, the new pink kind, the only ones like them in town. There are only two houses in this section so far, the Stehle's two-story brick job and the Model Home with the weedy lawn. They sit next to each other all alone, like farmhouses.

The Camaro makes so much noise that we pull over a full block away, on the far side of the empty lot across the street. The lot has tall weeds and tough old renegade corn up to a man's waist, and when we get out and walk to the middle I look back at the car. The street is low and the car sits in the hollow of the curb facing west, back the way we came. The last of the light catches the windshield, highlighting the crack that cuts the passenger-side corner.

On the other side of us the Stehle house catches the same evening light on the upper-story windows, and they glow purple at the top and gold at the bottom. We walk closer across the field, the hairy weeds cutting across our thighs and leaving burrs in the cuffs of my jeans. At the edge of the property we stop and sit on a concrete slab that covers a sewer entrance. The slab is so new that the concrete is still white, and has crisp edges. Bobby looks at his watch.

"We'll wait five minutes," he says.

All of the windows in the house are covered by beige-colored drapes, and there are no lights at all to be seen inside. There aren't any cars in the driveway, no toys or tools or pets in the yard. It looks the way a house does when the owners are away on vacation.

"There's not even anyone home," I whisper. "Maybe we should just go."

"Yeah," Bobby says, louder than me. "We should, probably." He leans forward and unties his shoe, then reties it, then does the whole thing over again. I watch him, waiting for him to get to his feet, and I think about Connie, trying to picture her, and I'm not able to, or Stacey either. It's as though they had both been wiped out of my memory. Their house doesn't even look like the same house Bobby and I have driven past a thousand times, with Bobby staring straight ahead rather than let on he's out on this dead-end street to see anybody. The house could be anywhere, home to anyone.

It's then that I see it: from left to right the top right window is growing blacker as the curtain is drawn open. I hear

Bobby take in his breath a hitch, and then the curtain stops, halfway to the other side.

There is just enough light from the west to make out the girl behind the glass. It's Connie; I can see her blond hair as the last bit of the sun catches it around the edges, but her body is dark, and her face is hidden behind a purple reflected glare. Bobby gets to his feet and starts walking across the street toward the house. I follow him, wondering why we're not slinking along rather than just walking, and I try to walk the way Bobby walks: upright, like we had every right to be where we were, but my back bows and my feet swing under me too quickly.

We stop in the Stehle's yard next to a small birch tree that isn't even as tall as I am, and I stand behind it, using what little of it there is for cover. We're close enough to see that Connie—just like Paula said she would be—is staring out the window, but not down at us; instead she's looking out over the field toward where we left the car. I turn and look back, but in the dark I can only see the very top of the Camaro's roof, where the vinyl is peeling.

Up in the window Connie stands with her shoulders sort of down and her hips forward, the way kids will when they're told to stand still. I can see her hollow, dark-rimmed eyes and her little pink mouth that hangs slightly open. When I bring my eyes down to her chest, I see that one of her small breasts is mottled with purple and blue and yellow, and she has two long bruises like whiplashes that go from her stomach around her side and up under her arm. The other side of her—the right side—is pale and unmarked, and I can see the small dent where her hipbone pokes out, and the long, curving line of muscle that will end down below the windowsill, between her legs.

As I watch her, she raises her right hand and for a second I think she's going to wave at somebody, somebody out on the street behind us, but instead she just scratches her cheek, with all four fingers curled, in the way a baby would—more pushing at her face than scratching it—all the while still gazing out across the field.

Then, in front of my eyes, Bobby starts to jump. He jumps up and down, waving his arms crazily over his head. When she looks down and sees him, he stops and motions with his hands for her to come down. *Come on*, he mouths, jerking his head to the side toward the street, *come on*. She stares at him for the longest time, and he doesn't stop for a second, all the way up until the curtains fall closed.

He stops dead and just stares at the window, his hands down at his side, breathing heavy. He stares that way for a while, and finally he turns to me, shaking his head a little. His face is scary to look at; it almost glows in the dark. He looks the way I saw a man look in church once, after he'd run up to the front and fallen to his knees, crying, in the middle of the doxology. But we all just kept singing, *Praise God from whom all blessings flow* . . .

"Did you see her?" he says. He looks back up at the window, then again at me. "Did you see that?"

Then the door opens right in front of us and Connie comes a step out onto the stoop, still naked, smiling with her

183

hand shading her eyes from the porch light. Above her ear there is a white patch where they must have shaved her skull. I can see the black crosshatched tracks of the thread and even the dark fuzz of new hair coming in around it. She looks wobbly.

"Hello?" she says. It sounds like she's talking into a bad telephone connection. "Hello?" Inside the house a single lamp is on; I can hear a TV close by. Somewhere a cabinet door slams.

"Honey?" she says then, peering harder out into the dark. "Stace?" My blood goes suddenly cool and I start to back up, one foot at a time, down the sidewalk toward the street. She takes a few steps off the porch and Bobby walks up to her and whispers something in her ear. I don't hear it so I don't know why she smiles at him the way she does, but that smile does it. I turn around and run back toward the field, my feet making big slapping noises on the pavement. I hit the field and don't stop. Ahead of me in the next street Bobby's Camaro sits, completely dark now. As I get close the street lamp above it flickers on, pink and uncertain, and I see with a little shiver that there's the shadow of a girl sitting in the passenger seat. The first thing I think is Oh God, it *is* Stacey Stehle come back, but then I realize that it's Paula, and the way she sits makes me think back to the seventh grade when I would watch her climb into those cars after school.

"Stretch," she'd said to me then, "you know why older guys like junior-high girls?" When I shook my head she smiled a little, but a serious smile that I remember showed nothing but absolute confidence. She said, "Because they *give*, that's why."

When I get up close to the car I see, after all, that I was wrong, and there's nobody in it, just the two empty high-backed seats. I climb in and the vinyl is cold to the touch, and stiff. Bobby has left the key in the ignition, but when I twist it the car roars so loud underneath I have to switch it off. I sit in it and wait, and after a while the windows fog over, like someone laid a pink blanket over the windshield. I start to shiver and I can't stop; after a while I just quit trying.

another
pyramid
scheme

When the Reverend died my old man lost his job, and the closest he ever got to getting another was when he dragged encyclopedias around town in the back of his green Maverick. The Reverend was my older brother; he drowned when he was fourteen and I was twelve. I remember him leaving for the pool with his towel rolled up like a sausage and his combination lock in his fist. I remember my mother yelling *Take your sister* but he just ignored her and kept going.

What I remember most, though, is my old man changing. He started hanging around the kitchen smoking and blowing his nose. He didn't speak to me unless he had to. He bought the two identical Mavericks and when they came to take one of them away he started arguing with them about which one was paid for and which one wasn't. It didn't really matter though, a little while later the same two guys came and took the other one. One of them smiled at me, rubbing his nose, and told me I was pretty. When I smiled back he rubbed it harder.

The next summer my mother made me take swimming lessons twice a week in the morning. I took them alone at the falling-apart city pool, from a guy so old he had no waist, hips or rear—his skinny legs hung straight down out of his belly.

He gave me all of two lessons before he died in his sleep. One of the lifeguards took over the lessons; a chunky high-school boy with a pug nose. His name was Les Plinck. When he told me his name I laughed out loud and he laughed along with me. He said it sounds like gasoline additive, doesn't it? It was a pretty nice laugh. Before I knew what I was doing I'd let him teach me the backstroke and even let him teach me the crawl. After my old man lost the two Mavericks and couldn't drive me anymore, Les Plinck started picking me up at the corner in his dad's beat-up old car. I could have walked but I let him drive me just the same. I hoped people would see me but they never did, which was okay, because the car wasn't so nice and Les Plinck wasn't really much of a prize.

At the same time my folks had gotten involved with an outfit called SuccessfuLife. They covered the kitchen table with SuccessfuLife literature from a black ring-binder. If I picked any of it up, the old man came over and took it out of my hands without a word. Most of the stuff was just pictures of couples with their names, cities, and levels printed beneath them. Near the top were Rick and Helen Jordan/Alton, Illinois/Silver Level. Alton was just close enough to get my parents excited about the possibilities. They made me take their photograph together against the garage door. They wore their funeral clothes and tried to smile the way successful people might.

The Reverend had been a polite kid; too polite for my folks, who were made nervous by polite people. They called him the

Reverend to make fun of him and get him to knock it off but he never did. He got straight A's and played the bassoon, both of which were embarrassing to my folks. He cleaned out their ashtrays and raked the shag carpet and raised two gerbils named George and Martha. When Martha had babies he came and got me, all excited. I peeked into the cage and screamed. I was looking straight down into a gerbil baby; George had eaten its head off. The Reverend gave the both of them away after that. He didn't get any more pets.

The Reverend drowned in the deep end, very quietly. Nobody used the deep end after they took off the diving board; and since the lifeguards only used the one chair at the shallow end, it left a blind spot behind the joint of the L, where the pool turns to the right. Nobody noticed the Reverend go down. When the lifeguard found him he was at the bottom, up against the drain where the filter had tugged him. Nobody could figure out what he had been doing over there, no splashing, no playing, so quiet no one could hear him.

As a test Les Plinck asked me to tread water in the middle of the deep end for three minutes with my fingers in the air. Each time my ears dipped underwater I could hear the sound of the pool filter drumming close against my skull, and I kicked hard to get my head up. I knew that sound was the last sound the Reverend had ever heard but I didn't let it scare me. It did not beckon me to my death. It did not sing to me of other worlds. It just sounded like the pool filter at the bottom of the stupid Municipal Pool. I figured I would tread

191

water for the three minutes and then do five or six more, but I only made it to two before Les Plinck blew his whistle and ordered me out. His face was white and his fingers trembled on the whistle—from then on the deep end was out of bounds.

My old man called up the Silver Level Jordans to invite them over to the house. He listened to the receiver and said, no, he'd rather they came over here so he could be hospitable and not put them out. He said, no, he really couldn't put them out, he couldn't barge in on them. He didn't mention anything about not having a car. My mother cupped her hand next to her mouth and said *Tell them for cocktails* but my old man turned his shoulder away from her and made the date. When he hung up the phone his hair fell into his eyes and he left it there. His hair was thin and gray-brown, like old wire, and it also poked out of the bridge of his nose and in little tufts from his ears. I sometimes wondered how he could hear, or even if it mattered.

The Jordans arrived forty-five minutes late; my old man spent most of the time in the bathroom, running the taps. My mother raked the carpet back and forth in front of the couch, doing her best to get the nap up. She'd used spot cleaner on it and the room smelled like hairspray. When he finally arrived, Jordan filled the doorway. He was huge, black-haired. His wife stood behind him, off the stoop, since there was no room for her on it with him there. Behind her their Cadillac stuck out of our driveway and into the street. A toy cocker spaniel with jewelled eyes sat on the shelf behind the rear window.

"Pleasure," my mother said, blinking up at Jordan. When he came into the living room his shadow left the doorway and let in some sun, but then he crossed over and blotted out what little light came through the picture window. My old man came out from the bathroom with a wild look in his eyes. Jordan saw him and smiled.

"Robert," he said, "I feel like I know you already."

es Plinck was an Eagle Scout. Les Plinck played sophomore football and intramural basketball. Les Plinck listened to Z-Rock 97. Les Plinck had been an Honorary March of Dimes Bat Boy at Busch stadium, against the Dodgers. Les Plinck had even talked to Stan the Man at his restaurant, Stan Musial & Biggie's. But Les Plinck had no car of his own. Les Plinck had no fake ID. Les Plinck had no girlfriend. Les Plinck was kind of fat.

Les Plinck sat on the edge of the pool and showed me the scar where he'd cracked open his head on the pool floor. Turned the whole shallow end pink, he said. I parted his wet hair and saw the line but didn't say anything. He reached back and put his finger on it. Right there, he said, can't you see it?

"I'm looking, stay still," I said. His head was big and his hair was soft, like a wet kitten's. He had a cowlick in the back;

a little black and white hurricane that drilled right into the back of his skull. The Reverend had had a cowlick.

"You got dandruff," I said, even though I didn't see any.

He moved away. "It's the chlorine." He left a wet stain on the concrete in the shape of his butt—a *big* wet stain.

"Mark Spitz doesn't have dandruff," I said.

"He's a fag, that's why."

That made me angry. Mark Spitz had been the Reverend's biggest hero. The Reverend had admired quiet, slim men who were clean-cut and excellent at something. He'd admired David Niven in *Around the World in Eighty Days*. Also Batman, but only as Bruce Wayne.

"Mark Spitz is *engaged*," I said. "You don't know anything about anything. You're stupid and fat and you got dandruff."

But Les Plinck had dived into the deep end, splashing too much on account of his weight. He started swimming laps and was still swimming them when I closed the gate behind me and started walking home.

very summer our street melted. You could push rocks down into the glossy black tar as if it were fudge. The city came by and spread gravel on it and that helped until the next year, when the fudge would bubble back up. They'd done that for so many years our street was high in the middle, bowed. Cars that parked along it sat at such a tilt that passenger doors were always getting stuck in the grass.

The Reverend used to walk to the library every day to

arrange the books. Somewhere he had learned the Dewey Decimal System, and when he went to the public library he found so many books out of order he took it upon himself to arrange them. My mother made him take me along. We walked down the soft street in the exact middle because our feet slid sideways out of our tire-tread sandals if we didn't. When a car came I grabbed his hand, but when the car passed and we went back out to the middle of the street he always let go. When I tried to put my arm around his shoulders the way the boys did, he squirmed until it slid off.

In the library I sat on a round stool by the window and watched the cars go by. I didn't know the system so I couldn't help. Once the librarian tried to interest me in some books about girls who have heroic adventures and problems with their parents. I left my gum in one of them that was titled *Dolly's Dilemma*. I switched the yellow cards in the rest of them, and put them back on the shelf in the wrong places. Some I slid behind the radiator.

The year before he died, the Reverend called me into his room for a conference. He sat on his bed in his underwear, surrounded by encyclopedias. He was a skinny kid but I never noticed it back then. He was playing his Swingle Singers records, where the people sang but didn't use any words. "Biddy diddy dee," they went. "Boddy doddy dah."

He picked up his glasses and put them onto his nose. "There are good people and bad people," he said. "A lot more bad than good."

I nodded. Lists filled my head.

195

"All the bad ones come out on top, just like in that saying."

"I'm good," I said.

"Our parents aren't," he said. "Good people don't act like that."

I thought of the whippings the Reverend had gotten from the old man, the screaming from behind the bedroom door; even later, when he was too good to whip but still got it anyway. He'd come out of the bedroom dirty-faced and grim, and right in front of them he'd start cleaning ashtrays.

"They don't mess with you," he said. I thought for a second that meant he agreed I was good. "I don't know. Maybe because you're a girl."

I didn't know what to say.

"Don't worry, Paula," he said. "You're just a kid. You got it made. He likes *you*."

rch your back," Les Plinck said, standing next to me in the shallow end. "Try to keep your whole chest out of the water. You can float that way for a long time, even with a cramp."

He showed me, arching his back over. His chest rose up and water streamed off the sides of him. It was like a sub coming up. When I arched my back he looked at my chest.

"Cut it out," I said, looking up into the sky.

"You're sinking." He put his hand under my shoulder blades. "Fill up with air and then only short breaths." I let him hold me up while I got my buoyancy right. At just the right arch and lung pressure I could float like a bubble. It was amazing. I rolled my eyes back and saw that Les was stroking my floating hair between the tips of his fingers; his eyelids were low and his mouth trembled.

I straightened up and put my feet back on the bottom. "Why do you always have to put your hands all over me?" I said. "What's your problem?"

He stepped away. Water swirled between us. "I want to make sure nothing happens to you," he said. "If you get afraid of the water, you never get over it."

"These lessons are a scam," I said. "You just want to feel me up. You're a creep, Lester Plinck."

He backed off another step. "It's Leslie," he said. He lowered himself into the water so all of him was covered but his head.

"You killed my brother, *Leslie*."

Water trickled down his face past his eyes, off his chin. "I was watching the window that day," he said. "I was checking baskets. By the time I got there it was too late."

"You take advantage," I said. I found the proper tone of voice. "People like you ruin the whole world."

He took a breath and disappeared under the water. His dark outline flowed away from me out to the deep end.

The Jordans stayed until after midnight explaining SuccessfuLife to my folks. I watched them for a while. They didn't touch any food or drink or my old man's cigarettes. Apparently SuccessfuLife was attached to some kind of holiday products

197

company. They sold everything that had to do with cele-
brations: candles, cards, wrapping paper, candy, mistletoe,
paper skeletons, red-white-and-blue Uncle Sam centerpieces,
plastic praying hands, Easter egg dye, green foil four-leaf
clovers and cardboard valentines. The Jordans hadn't brought
any of these things with them. They had a thick binder that
looked just like my folks' thick binder, except that theirs was
full of glossy pictures of SuccessfuLife products and order
forms.

"You'd send in your orders to me, I send them on to Salt
Lake," Jordan said. "Once you get fourteen couples under you,
you get to skip me altogether and send all of your folks' orders straight through. My commission is over for good.
Period. We're out of your life forever."

"You can still come over," my mother said. My old man
nodded.

"Let's go over the forms a second, here," Jordan said.

Sometime that evening the door to my bedroom opened
and Jordan leaned in.

"I'm figuring out this isn't the way to the bathroom," he
said.

I was sitting on my bed, playing some of the Reverend's
records. The music was loud enough that he couldn't have
mistaken it for the bathroom. "Behind you back there," I said.

He didn't move right away. "Bet you anything that's a
fake tongue on that fella there," he said, pointing to one of my
posters taped to the wall. "It's got to be plastic or rubber, I

bet." I didn't say anything. I had stacked nine records on my phonograph spindle, and he had interrupted them.

"You probably got homework or something," he said.

"It's summer," I said. "There's no school."

"I know that. I was pulling your leg." He stood there and watched me for a verse or two.

"What do you do all day in the summer?" he said.

"Nothing, anymore," I said. "I take swimming lessons Tuesday and Thursday mornings. I watch TV."

"You ought to help your old man out, you know," he said. "Get him going out of the blocks. Help him fill out his roster."

"Uh-huh," I said.

"That's the difference, you know. The ones that come out on top always have the support of the family."

"All I have to do is help, and he'll get a car like yours, right?"

He nodded. "Could very well be," he said. Something in his face made him look like he believed it. He pushed the door shut behind him. "You like cars?"

I felt suddenly warm. He took a step forward and I saw that somehow he had come to be standing just in front of me. He was so big he was all I could see.

"I like some," I said. I pulled my legs up under me.

His eyes flicked out to the street and then back down at me. "How do you get to these swimming lessons of yours?" he said.

"My father drives me."

He looked at me for a second or two, like there was some kind of secret just between us, and then before I knew it he was back at the door with his hand on the knob.

"Someday we can go for a ride, then," he said. "Let you see a nice car close up." I didn't say anything. The door closed behind him just as a new record dropped.

Three days later it was the Reverend's birthday, or would have been. My mother got picked up by her cousins to spend the day resting at their trailer in the country. The old man floated around the house like a dead body in a current. I tracked him down in the kitchen.

"Hey, Poppa," I said. "I want to buy something off you."

He was sitting at the table in front of his black binder. He looked up at me and squinted.

"What are you going on about?" he asked. It was the most he'd said to me in weeks.

"Your stuff," I said. "I want to buy something for the Reverend's birthday. A card or a party hat or something."

He took in a few breaths like he was winded, and then went back to looking at his book. His hair fell over his eyes and he left it there. "It takes three to four weeks," he said. "You're not allowed to keep an inventory until you're up to Bronze."

"Oh," I said. "Maybe something for the Fourth of July?"

He closed the binder. "What are you talking about?" he said, rubbing his eyes with his thumb and forefinger. He took his hands away from his face and stared at me.

"I don't know," I said. "I mean, aren't you selling this stuff now? The stuff in the book?"

"Jesus, not to *ourselves*," he said. "There's no money in that. That's not the goal." He'd gotten suddenly red in the face. "That's for the folks *under* us. Our Success Force."

"I was just trying to help."

"Well," he said, a little softer. "I wish you were in school right now. That's where you could help."

"I hate school," I said. "I hate everything."

He wasn't listening. He stared out the picture window at the empty driveway.

"See, then you could put up flyers in the cafeteria," he said. "Leave things around where teachers could see them. That's where you could help."

"Mr. Jordan gave me a ride to my swimming lesson," I said.

"I need to fill out my roster, is what *I* need."

"Les Plinck was late and Mr. Jordan was waiting in his car down at the corner."

He sniffed and scowled and rubbed his nose. "Teachers are always needing stuff like this for the holiday windows and walls and all of that. You could cover the whole school with this stuff. Top to bottom."

"Les Plinck was late," I repeated, but he still didn't hear me. "And then there was nobody at the pool but me. I could have *drowned*."

But he had opened the binder again and was staring at it, biting his lip and sniffling. His nose had begun to run. I looked out at the driveway. A car drove past—a piece of green junk with an old woman inside. Only June and already you could hear its tires sticking to the tar on our street. It sounded like tearing cloth.

It was true, Les Plinck *had* been late, so I'd slipped into the water alone, out into the deep end. I went out to the middle to think; think about all those things the Reverend had said, all those things he'd been right about. I went out to where the Reverend had gone down and I filled up my lungs with air and floated there, my face in the sun. I floated so long I forgot where I was and nearly drifted off to sleep. When Les Plinck finally showed up and saw me floating there alone, he freaked. Nothing I said would console him.

Poor Les Plinck. Poor fat Leslie. He was too late to save the Reverend and he was too late, after all, to save me.

guns
went
Off

Lorraine is checking a hole in her white nylon stocking. It's just above the ankle, above the rim of her white sneaker. Next to the hole there's a spot of blood from someone in the next room. It doesn't seem to bother her.

"Chris, do you really remember me?" She leans forward in the vinyl chair when she asks the question. "I mean, I know you remember me but do you remember everything? Everything that went on in high school and all?" She's a big one for talking about high school, Lorraine is. She loves to recall how she led me on and on, and how she ended up marrying my best friend. I believe she counts it as an accomplishment in her life.

"I haven't had a head injury, Lorraine. I'm not a patient here. Of course I remember."

She bends over to look again at the hole. "I'm just making conversation." She doesn't appear to notice the blood. "Ouch, will you look at that hole?"

Lorraine's husband and brother shot each other almost two years ago. Nobody knows why. Lorraine says they were cleaning their guns out on the deck and they just went off. The two men were taken to separate hospitals. Her husband hung on for a week and then died suddenly. She was caught on the road between hospitals and wasn't there when he expired (her word). Her brother, Fuzzy, survived and was never charged by anybody with anything.

Her husband—my best friend in high school—was Les Plinck. Les had been the Illinois state trap-shooting champion at age thirteen, whereupon he retired. He was on the chubby side. His nickname had been Boom-Boom until he got so big they started calling him Boom-Boom-Boom. Although many had tried, nobody had ever come up with a very funny tag line for the joke, "What goes Boom Boom Boom Plinck?"

Lorraine pulls the stocking away from her ankle with her thumb and forefinger, raising a sheer white tent. Before she lets it snap back I imagine the color of the skin beneath it, although the proper term would be remember.

Before last night, the only time Lorraine had let me touch that skin was twelve years ago, before she was married, on a night that Les Plinck was out of town at a gun show. It was over quickly and quietly—a sad and disappointing event all around—and we never mentioned it, even to each other. I left town a few weeks later to go back to college and never returned; not for their wedding, not for Les's funeral. When two months after the shooting Lorraine wrote me that she'd started nursing school, I wasn't surprised. It was something she had always wanted to do, she wrote. No connection whatsoever. I never answered the letter, either.

I look around the waiting room. "It's so quiet here," I say. "Time must drag when there's nothing to do."

She snorts. "There's always plenty to do. We get plenty of traffic." She laughs again. "Hey, that's not bad, plenty of traffic."

I point to the blood on her stocking. "Will that come out in the washing machine?"

She laughs. "It's easy to see you've never been married, sweetie."

"Lorraine, tell me something. I read somewhere that the gang kids wear the clothes their friends were shot in. Some kind of honor thing."

"Let me tell you about bullet holes. The hardest thing about bullet holes are the tiny pieces of cloth that get in the wound. The dyes are poisonous." She lets the cuff of her white slacks back down over her ankle. "Chris, if it looks like you're going to be shot, the best thing you can do is strip."

"I've always counted on using that time to run away."

She doesn't even smile. "They cut the clothes off with these big scissors. There's only rags left. Plus the colored kids have too much style to wear holes in their clothes."

"They like guns, that's for sure."

"No, they don't. That's baloney. That's TV bullshit. I was married to someone who loved guns, remember."

I stand up. "I should go. I want to talk to Fuzzy."

"What?" she says. She smooths her white slacks over her thighs. "Why?"

"I need to ask him something."

"You shouldn't. You'll just get him in trouble at work."

"I won't. I just need his help with something."

She walks up to me and brushes the hair from my eyes. Her hand smells like rubbing alcohol. "At least bring home some dinner tonight," she says. "Make yourself useful while you're here, whatever it is you're doing. Earn your keep."

"Funny," I say.

I locate Fuzzy down at the athletic field. He's riding the high school's mowing tractor in long ovals—each one a slightly smaller version of the inside of the running track, until he finishes it off in a single swipe like the last stroke of a straight razor. Back in high school Fuzzy had white mad-professor hair that grew in tufts: one in back, one on top, and one over each ear. Fuzzy once threatened me with a knife; I think if we'd had guns back then he would have used one. Maybe not on me, but on someone.

But age seems to have mellowed Fuzzy. Older, thicker, his top tuft retreating, he looks almost gentle—that is, until he runs the mower over the metal rim of the running track and kills the motor.

Shit piss fuck cocksucker motherfucker and tits. The words drift up to me in the parking lot. He used to say the same thing—the same stream of curses—back in high school, for fun, to make an impression. Fifteen years later they sound quaint.

When he drives the mower up the path I wave him down and explain my problem. He listens over the idle of the mower with a sweet expression of confusion. It occurs to me that he may not remember who the hell I am. It could also be that he's hungover.

"Let me see them," he says when I'm done. I reach into my pocket and pull out three plastic film canisters, keeping them in my palm. Inside are my little brother's ashes—at least my share of them. His wife's family divvied them up as if they were gold dust. Since my brother and I were technically es- tranged, they considered themselves his real family—they kept most of his ashes and all of his wife's. The two of them were killed when their Cessna crashed and burned some- where outside of Seattle.

"You got me, guy," he says after a moment. "Maybe dump them in the locker room someplace."

"Somebody will just mop him up, there, Fuzz. Probably you."

Fuzzy shades his eyes and looks toward the highway. "How about the baseball field? He like baseball?"

"He'll just get mowed."

"Shit, man, I don't know." He reaches down to rev up the mower.

"Come on, Fuzz, I've got to put him somewhere. Can you get me on the roof?"

"Not allowed."

"It's summer. Who cares?"

"Squeege cares."

Squeege was our principal. "He's still here?"

"The guy's all right," says Fuzzy. "He's not a bad guy when you get to know him."

"Wow. I can't believe this is the same old Fuzzy saying this."

"Come on, already," says Fuzzy. He climbs off the tractor and walks off toward the gym. His gait is almost bowlegged; a mower-riding cowboy.

Up on the roof the afternoon sun hits hotter and brighter than down below. Cooling vents seem to have sprouted like mushrooms and they rotate slowly, the metal fins flashing. I can see the floor plan of the entire school spread out around me, the angles and corners all simple up here, as if I were standing on an extremely tall foundation. The entire building shudders with energy.

"This is very cool," I say to Fuzzy. I walk to the edge and look out over the soccer field—small white pebbles stick to my shoes. "You can see everything from up here. How come I never did this before?"

Fuzzy has his enormous key chain stretched out from his hip, and absently fondles the keys at the end of it. "Get expelled, that's why," he says.

"I don't know, I think Richie could spend eternity up here. What do you think?"

Fuzzy shrugs. "Up to you, guy."

"No, I guess not," I say after a moment. "He'd just get washed off first time it rains." I slide the film canisters back into my pockets.

Fuzzy looks pained. "Look, did he ever say he wanted to be spread or whatever around here?"

"No, he hated it here. Couldn't wait to leave. He went into the Air Force and got his GED in some missile silo in South Dakota or someplace like that."

Fuzzy is incredulous now. "Fuck, man, you mean to tell me the guy never even graduated from here?"

"Look, his wife's family is going to spread their half somewhere on an Air Force base I've never even been to. Some runway or hangar or something."

"That sounds pretty cool," Fuzzy says. "I'd just lump my part in with theirs."

"You think so, Fuzz? I'm not so sure."

"Well, it beats whatever the hell you're doing, man." He swings his keys. The chain wraps around his wrist; he swings them the other direction to unwind it.

"So what did they do with Les?" I say.

Fuzzy's keys land in his palm. "I don't know anything about that."

"He was cremated, right? I mean, I heard he was."

Fuzzy shades his eyes and looks out over the soccer field, as if he just remembered he had important duties. "I better get back to work, guy," he says. "The Squeege is a bastard about taking breaks."

"Yeah, you don't want to lose this job, Fuzz. Not with this terrific roof access and all."

He stares at me for a second, maybe trying to resurrect the old Fuzzy, then walks away toward the roof door. His keys smack against his thighs with each step.

"Hey, Fuzz," I say. "You want to see the ashes?"

He stops but doesn't turn around. He says no, but so low I almost can't hear.

"Anytime, Fuzz," I say. He holds the door and I walk ahead of him downstairs and back out to his tractor.

"So, listen," I say as he climbs onto the seat. "Maybe you can think about a good place and we'll try again tomorrow, how does that sound?"

He works the gearshift. "Tomorrow's Saturday."

"Okay, Monday. I'll come check you out on Monday, same time." I roll the film canisters around in my palm, then shove them into my jacket.

His eyes follow them the way a dog follows a biscuit. He fires up the mower and twists the steering wheel hard to one side. It chugs forward with a jerk that seems to whip along his spine. I spot something lying on the asphalt path: it's a tightly rolled cellophane baggie, long and narrow and silver-gray.

"Fuzzy," I say. "Hey, Fuzz. You dropped your weed."

I point to the sidewalk and he swings the mower around, cruises up next to it, and snatches the baggie without slowing down. He heads off to do the soccer field, bouncing on the black vinyl seat.

See you Monday, I say to myself. Murderer.

Lorraine is on the phone when I tap on her screen door and let myself in. She's still in her hospital-white slacks. There's a pitcher of lemonade sitting on the counter in a puddle and a plastic bottle of vodka next to it. By the time she hangs up the phone I've made myself a glass and freshened it twice.

She picks up her own glass and swirls it. "That was Erin on the phone," she says. "I don't know what you did today, but Fuzzy's after you now. He stopped by the package store and he told Erin while she was ringing him up. He said he was going to take care of you."

"Well, I think you've been misinformed. I spent a very pleasant hour with Mr. Fuzzy today. He seemed friendly enough to me."

"I'm just telling you what Erin said."

"What were her exact words?"

"I can't remember her exact words. Like I said, Fuzzy's after you. You better stay away from him."

"Well, I'm not afraid of Fuzzy. I'm not in high school anymore."

"You might wish you were if you're not careful."

"Funny. Hey, why don't we go upstairs and take a shower?"

"I don't want to take a shower and don't try to change the subject. You're always doing that." She picks up a lemon half and squeezes it over the pitcher, but she's already exhausted this particular lemon half and nothing comes out but a couple of seeds. She drops it in the sink and wipes the back of her hand across her forehead. "Plus it's too hot," she says.

"Then we'll take a cool bath."

"I'm too tense."

"It'll soothe you."

"Look, it's too hot to come up with any more excuses. No shower, no bath, all right?" She dumps a half-empty glass into the sink. "Not to mention the fact you didn't bring home anything to eat like I asked."

I sit on the counter and drink from my glass. "Jesus," I say after a minute. "What's Fuzzy's problem? What am I to him?"

"He's always hated you."

"I know that. I had to live through it."

"Then what's your question?"

"My question is what the hell for?"

She pours herself another glass of lemonade. She fills the glass to the top and forgets to add any liquor. "He says he's going to shoot you in the forehead and piss in the hole." She giggles.

"He was drunk. He was trying to impress Erin."

She shakes her head. "He wasn't drunk and he was only there to buy cigarettes."

"You seem to remember a lot more now. If he's so mad, why didn't he say something to me this morning?"

"Maybe he did. Did you say anything to upset him?"

"Nothing."

Her look is steady. "So what did you talk about?"

"Sports."

"Sports," she says. "You better watch yourself, bud."

Several hours later I open my eyes to Lorraine's reading light. It feels like the middle of the night, but it's still early, maybe eleven-thirty.

I put my hand on her hipbone. "I had a dream you were on the phone," I say.

"Fuzzy wants to talk to you." She hands me the receiver.

Fuzzy's voice has been chemically altered. "Dipshit. Fuckwad. I'm going to fuck you up." It sounds like he's in a bar. There's music in the background and voices. Somebody drops a trayful of glassware—that or hits a nice hard break on a pool table.

"Who is this again?" I say.

"This is me, bastard mother shithead."

"Jesus, Fuzz," I say. "You're so fucked up you can't even cuss right."

"Who do you think you are, shitface? What did you come back here for, anyway?"

"Come talk to me in the morning, Fuzz. Go home and go to sleep." I hand the receiver back to Lorraine, who's lying on her side facing me. She hangs it up behind her without turning over.

I look at her closed eyelids. "You know, maybe I should ask whose side you're on in all this."

Lorraine shrugs and turns away from me.

"This is the same man who killed my best friend," I say. "This should be taken into consideration."

She turns her head back slightly in my direction. "You heard about that? Strange how it had slipped my mind . . ."

"Funny. You know, it's me who should be taking care of him."

"All you have to do is avoid him. Stay out of his way. Leave him alone from here on out."

"I'm serious. He should watch himself."

"Yeah?" she says. "Well, my money's on Fuzz."

"That's a great thing to say." I stretch my hand over her head to turn off her reading light but I can't reach it without climbing over her. I pull my arm back, awkwardly, to my side. "You know, I wonder about you sometimes," I say.

"Wonder what?"

"I don't know; what you think, how you feel about things. You're kind of cold, to tell you the truth."

She draws in a breath. "Look, if you don't like it, leave. Take off again."

"I'm planning to. I've been nothing but clear on that. As soon as I do this thing I have to do, I'm out of here."

She turns out the light. "Don't let the door smack you on the ass on your way out."

"Funny," I say.

When I wake up Lorraine is already downstairs dressed for work. Today she wears a boxy white dress uniform, considerably less sexy than the previous day's slacks.

"Fuzzy called back this morning," she says, dumping the contents of the coffee pot into the sink.

"Tell him apology accepted."

"He said to tell you you're a shitwad piece of crap," says

Lorraine. "He's going to shoot your fingers off and jam them up your ass one by one."

"Jesus. What's his problem?"

Lorraine smooths her white dress absently, then twists and examines the back. "I'm only telling you what he told me," she says.

"He's schizo. He's at least two distinct people."

"He's just Fuzzy. There's nothing wrong with him that wasn't always wrong with him."

"Easy for you to say. He's your brother. He'd never threaten you like this."

"Funny," she says.

I sit down on a kitchen stool. "He actually might shoot me. I can't believe someone wants to shoot me."

"It happens. Guns go off all the time. You get used to it." She rinses the plates and slides them into the dishwasher. She flips the catch and the machine starts to grind. She leans back against it and looks at me with sudden tenderness.

"Hey, enough of this, let's you and me take a shower," she says. "Clean up our act. I've got time."

"Now you're being nice? What's in it for me?"

"You figure it out."

"All right," I say. "If you want." I'm beginning to think it might be a good idea to stay as far inside the house as possible, away from the windows.

In the shower I soap the entirety of Lorraine's back, especially the two small dents above her tailbone. She leans away from me with her hands and elbows flat against the tile and her toes gripping the rubber appliqué flowers on the tub floor. She breathes heavily through her nose; her shoulder blades push back against my fingers.

"Lorraine," I say. "You never told me where Les's ashes were scattered."

"You're right, I never did."

"It might help me finish what I have to do."

"Well, I'll tell you one thing," she says. "They're not in here."

"Funny. You happen to have Les's old pistol lying around?"

She stands up straight but doesn't turn around. "What, so you can use it on my brother? I think you've been watching too much TV. Enough is enough with this."

"It was just a thought. Forget it," I say. "Besides, it didn't seem to help Les any."

She stiffens, almost rising up onto her toes. "Don't touch that," she says. "I can clean there, thank you very much."

When she leaves for work I start in on the bedroom. She keeps lots of things in cardboard file boxes; they're mostly paper, but I take my time and go through everything. A lot of nursing school papers, blue-lettered, mimeographed at various slight angles. Credit card bills, warrantees, instructions for a microwave oven, and at the bottom of one, inexplicably, an electric breast pump. Across the room there's a drawer full of cash-register receipts, a small box with earrings, and an outdated prescription bottle, the typed letters smudged and faint. And under a stack of stained table napkins, a chrome-plated pistol.

I lift it out of the drawer. It's heavy; it smells the way hand tools smell when they've been left on a workbench all winter—a sharp and oily smell. I can't figure out how to release the cylinder, so I count the copper-snouted bullets from the front. I count four of the five visible, plus maybe the sixth in the chamber—I pull the hammer back slightly and yes, it's in there. Five bullets of a possible six. Was the sixth one removed from Fuzzy? My dead friend's gun is a heavy weapon and I have to heft it with both hands.

A car door slams below me in the driveway. I pull the shade back from the window and look down; it's Fuzzy, carrying a rifle one-handed, hunter style, his fist wrapped around the stock and the barrel pointed at the ground. He walks around the house and enters the fenced-in backyard through the high wooden gate. I cross the bedroom to the rear window. I see Fuzzy step up onto the low wooden deck and stand looking out away from the house.

I watch him for a few minutes and he doesn't do anything but stand there staring. After a while I carry the pistol downstairs. I carry the pistol to the kitchen and then out the kitchen door onto the deck behind Fuzzy. I raise the pistol just barely and clear my throat.

Fuzzy turns around without any special determination. The rifle barrel points at the deck near my feet.

"What's up, Fuzz," I say. "What's going on?"

He shrugs. The rifle barrel rises and falls with his shoulders. "Nothing's going on."

"Oh, so you just stopped by? You just happened to wander by here carrying a rifle?"

He shifts his weight, raising the barrel of the gun slightly, at about the level of my knees. "You told me to come by in the morning, so here I am."

"Oh," I say. "Now you came because I told you to."

He shrugs. "You've been saying things about me," he says. "Like you're going to take care of me for what happened to Les."

"What? Who told you that?"

"Jesus Christ, man, it was an accident," he says. His voice is suddenly strained. He looks wobbly, as though he might any second fall to his knees.

"No one believes me, man, but it was. We were just sitting out here getting high, and then he said something and I said something, then it was like we had these nasty animals in our hands, man, and they just started barking at each other, just snapping, like. I can't explain it any better." He pauses at this outburst and then shrugs again. "Nobody believes me." He shakes his head and wobbles a bit.

"Jesus, Fuzzy, exactly how much have you smoked already today? How fucked up are you?"

"None," he says. Only then does he seem to notice Les's pistol in my hand. He raises the rifle a little more, not quite at my chest but close. "That's his fucking pistol," he says. His eyes narrow as if he'd just then noticed I was there. "Man-oh-man," he says, "what did I ever do to you?"

"Jesus, Fuzzy." My pistol is pointed at his sternum. I can't recall raising it. "You threatened me over the phone last night. You threatened to kill me."

A couple of seconds pass, then he lowers the rifle, just a hair. "Yeah, but she told me to say all that," he says.

"She did what?"

"She called the bar and told me what to say. And I didn't say anything about fucking killing you, either. She must have made that shit up."

"She made that up? Shooting off my fingers? Pissing in my skull? Why? What the hell for?"

"Got me. Guess she wants to get rid of you, guy."

He raises the rifle again and his eyes are suddenly sharper. The wobble is gone. "Hey, no way," he says. "Fuck this. You drop yours first and then I'll drop mine. I been shot with that fucker once before already."

"Fuzzy," I say. "Fuzzy, listen to me. It's not between us. We don't actually have a problem with each other, do we?" The pistol—still pointing at Fuzzy's hairline—is heavy, starting to sag, and there is a small growing ache between my shoulder blades.

Fuzzy says nothing. His eyes are slits.

"Fuzzy," I say, "Fuzzy, listen to me . . . we both drop on three. Okay? On three."

Fuzzy wastes no time. "One two three," he says, lowering

the barrel of the rifle. I drop my arms and the action takes me all the way to my knees. I lean forward and place the pistol sideways on the deck, the barrel pointing at ten o'clock. Fuzzy takes this opportunity to raise his rifle barrel until it's even with my throat.

"Not so fast," he says.

"Oh, Jesus." My throat starts to close up. My bowels churn briefly and then go cold.

"Give me the ashes, chief."

"Jesus, Fuzzy," I say. "Don't bullshit me."

Fuzzy waves the nose of the rifle toward the edge of the deck. "You came here to dump them, right? So I'll just dump them right here and then you can get the flying fuck out of town."

I pull the three film canisters out of my pockets, mumbling protests that even I don't pay attention to. I place them on the deck next to the pistol and lean back on my heels. Fuzzy kneels and picks them up, then immediately pours one into his palm.

"Holy shit," he says, softly. "This is just like sand." The barrel of the rifle droops, as if in disappointment. He pours the handful onto the deck at his feet, then quickly empties the other two canisters. A tiny gray mound forms, dribbling silently through a crack between the boards.

As I watch I hear the sound of Lorraine's car drift over the fence, the jerk of her emergency brake, a door slam. Fuzzy notices too, and seems to snap out of his trance. "Shit," he says.

He shoves the little pile of ash around with his toe, trying to force it between the cracks.

"I didn't go up to Seattle at all," I tell him, watching his toe. "I made her folks send me these Federal Express."

"No shit?" Fuzzy says, still working the ash.

"No shit. I decided to come here instead."

Fuzzy snorts. "Well you're running about one disaster behind, then, chief," Fuzzy says. "It was all over with here a long time ago. There's nothing more to see." He leans over and picks up the pistol. He goes to his knees at the edge of the deck and slides both guns under, like a boy hiding a *Playboy* under his mattress.

"You know, chief, we should never have done this," Fuzzy says over his shoulder. "She catches us together and there'll be hell to pay."

"I'll go out through the gate," I say. But I'm too late. Lorraine opens the kitchen door and steps out onto the deck. There's a bright streak of red on her white uniform, from her shoulder down across her waist, as if a bloody hand had reached up from below and raked across her entire front. She stops with her hand on the door frame but doesn't say anything.

"You came back to change," I say. "You were probably hoping you'd scared me off by now."

She doesn't answer. Beside me, Fuzzy is breathing heavily. After a moment Lorraine raises a hand to wipe a strand of hair from her forehead.

"There was an accident right in front of the hospital," she says. "I didn't even have time to put on my scrubs." She looks around at the deck and the backyard. Her eyes sweep over the spot where the guns lay barely hidden, over the remnants of gray ash on the boards, over the unmowed grass. Then she looks at the two of us.

"Jesus, I've been trying like hell to keep you two apart," she says. "What's going on here?"

"Nothing," I say.

"Just shooting the shit," says Fuzzy. "We're cool."

"Just saying good-bye," I say.

But she isn't listening. She's looking down at her clothes. "You know, this is just my luck," she says. "Everything else is in the laundry hamper. Now I'll be stuck wearing a dirty uniform the entire rest of the day."

She wipes at her front hopelessly, and with that motion she looks for a second, streaked with blood, like someone I remember; like maybe the person I had come to find. Someone who could still manage to be surprised when everything went horribly wrong.